CUSTOMS OF THE COUNTRY

The sunlight touched William's exposed body so that it appeared to shimmer with a golden glow. He was smooth and almost totally devoid of bodily hair, apart from the boyish fluff that covered his legs. James sketched with animated pencil strokes, feeling as if the tip of the pencil were actually his hand, exploring and intruding on William's most intimate places. This was so much more interesting, thought James, than painting trees and hills and lifeless things.

He etched the shape of his model's body, following the lines of the torso and waist, shading in the taut flesh of his stomach. James did not dare to think about what the lad would look like completely naked; even this brief display was enough to make his underwear stick up, slippery and hot. He tried to conceal his excitement, not wanting to alarm William.

CUSTOMS OF THE COUNTRY

Rupert Thomas

First published in Great Britain in 1998 by
Idol
an imprint of Virgin Publishing Ltd
332 Ladbroke Grove
London W10 5AH

ISBN 0 352 33246 8

Cover photograph by Colin Clarke Photography

Typeset by SetSystems Ltd, Saffron Walden, Essex
Printed and bound in Great Britain by
Cox & Wyman Ltd, Reading, Berks

SAFER SEX GUIDELINES

These books are sexual fantasies – in real life, everyone needs to think about safe sex.

While there have been major advances in the drug treatments for people with HIV and AIDS, there is still no cure for AIDS or a vaccine against HIV. Safe sex is still the only way of being sure of avoiding HIV sexually.

HIV can only be transmitted through blood, come and vaginal fluids (but no other body fluids) – passing from one person (with HIV) into another person's bloodstream. It cannot get through healthy, undamaged skin. The only real risk of HIV is through anal sex without a condom – this accounts for almost all HIV transmissions between men.

Being Safe:
Even if you don't come inside someone, there is still a risk to both partners from blood (tiny cuts in the arse) and pre-come. Using strong condoms and water-based lubricant greatly reduces the risk of HIV. However, condoms can break or slip off, so:
* Make sure that condoms are stored away from hot or damp places.
* Check the expiry date – condoms have a limited life.
* Gently squeeze the air out of the tip.
* Check the condom is put on the right way up and unroll it down the erect cock.
* Use plenty of water-based lubricant (lube), up the arse and on the condom.
* While fucking, check occasionally to see the condom is still in one piece (you could also add more lube).
* When you withdraw, hold the condom tight to your cock as you pull out.

* Never re-use a condom or use the same condom with more than one person.
* If you're not used to condoms you might practise putting them on.
* Sex toys like dildos and plugs are safe. But if you're sharing them use a new condom each time or wash the toys well.

For the safest sex, make sure you use the strongest condoms, such as Durex Ultra Strong, Mates Super Strong, HT Specials and Rubberstuffers packs. Condoms are free in many STD (Sexually Transmitted Disease) clinics (sometimes called GUM clinics) and from many gay bars. It's also essential to use lots of water-based lube such as KY, Wet Stuff, Slik or Liquid Silk. Never use come as a lubricant.

Oral Sex:
Compared with fucking, sucking someone's cock is far safer. Swallowing come does not necessarily mean that HIV gets absorbed into the bloodstream. While a tiny fraction of cases of HIV infection have been linked to sucking, we know the risk is minimal. But certain factors increase the risk:
* Letting someone come in your mouth
* Throat infections such as gonorrhoea
* If you have cuts, sores or infections in your mouth and throat

So what is safe?
There are so many things you can do which are absolutely safe: wanking each other; rubbing your cocks against one another; kissing, sucking and licking all over the body; rimming – to name but a few.

If you're finding safe sex difficult, call a helpline or speak to someone you feel you can trust for support. The Terrence Higgins Trust Helpline, which is open from noon to 10pm every day, can be reached on 0171 242 1010.

Or, if you're in the United States, you can ring the Center for Disease Control toll free on 1 800 458 5231.

This is for

Emma
Fiona
Gareth
Scotty

Prologue

Gabriel sat apart from the others, quietly contemplating his shimmering reflection in the water below. He was pleased not to have to listen to the boys' endless chatter, each trying to better – by improbable story or outlandish lie – the others. Their words came across on the breeze to him muddled and distorted like the patter of distant feet; one could not tell their direction or the nature of their owner.

The river flowed, heavy and deep, the rocks and reeds at the bottom barely recognisable against the currents and mirror-like reflection from the late afternoon sun. Tranquil, yet never for a moment still, the water made its way endlessly downstream. Gabriel heard something splash into the water and he thought that maybe a fish had jumped out of the river and dropped back in again, or a kingfisher had dived below looking for its supper. Then the thought was gone and he returned to the world of his friends along the riverbank from him, who were throwing stones into the water.

'Oi, Gabe, what're you doing over there?' Tom called out. 'Come back and talk to us, you miserable sod.' Gabriel stuck his tongue out and gazed down at his own image in the water.

Tom shrugged his shoulders. 'Suit yourself.' He nudged his pal. 'What's up with him? Something we said?' The boy gave no answer.

Tank, as his mates called him, was nineteen years old and had spent his whole life in the village. His real name was Alfred Tankerd, but nobody addressed him as that, not even his own mother. He was shorter than the other boys, coming in at only five feet and six inches, but made up for this with his broad shoulders and sturdy thighs. His hair was as black as the Kent night and cropped close to his scalp. When he smiled his whole face lit up, eyes sparkling, teeth shining, and thick lips pulled far back over his gums. He looked like a bright young schoolboy, and reflected this in his cheeky, innocent manner.

Tank and Tom were best friends. They had lived in adjacent cottages when they were kids, gone to school together and had barely known their fathers, both of whom were killed in the war. They spent all their spare time together, down by the river in the secret barn. It was their place, they'd found it; everyone else was just a guest allowed to stick around, but only under their own strict terms.

A year older than his friend, Tom looked like an elongated version of Tank. The same short dark hair, piercingly bright eyes and thick lips curling upwards. He towered over his friend at nearly six feet. The only other difference was that his shoulders and hips were narrow and clearly defined, while Tank's were broad and sloping. Tom's buttocks compensated though, jutting out, round and tight, making his profile distinctly more masculine, more adult, than the other's. Gabriel thought the boys to be very handsome and loved to just sit near them and watch as they talked and played together.

The boys sat cross-legged, their trousers rolled up above their ankles, on the riverbank. From where he was situated Gabriel could see Charlie and Samuel beside the two lads with their feet dangling in the water, occasionally splashing each other or a passing swan. Both boys were eighteen and had not lived in

2

the village for as long as the others. Sam had moved with his mother and sisters only a year and a half ago. Charlie's family had settled in Rolvenden a year before that. They were extremely poor and had been forced to leave their fishing village and seek jobs as farm labourers. Charlie had been eager to make friends and was glad to be accepted by Tom and Tank even though they got up to all sorts of odd things.

He was a small lad and looked younger than his age. His features were petite and babyish: thin lips and pale blue eyes surrounded a delicate, turned-up nose. His skin was pale and lightly freckled, with a mop of wiry ash-blond hair on top. His torso was modest, but at the same time muscled and hard, with stiff nipples that forever poked out from under his shirt. There was a reserved quality that made him seem slightly withdrawn; a boy seeming to spend more time daydreaming than socialising. Tom was the one person who could arouse strong reaction in him. Charlie came alive, showed interest in the world, when Tom was around.

The boys splashed water up at one another with their feet and screamed hysterically with laughter, jostling, pushing and grasping in order to drag one another into the river.

'Watch it!' Tank shouted. Gabriel saw that he had been hit by a jet of water that Sam had intended for his companion. 'Can't you just sit quietly for a change?'

Samuel immediately stopped. 'Sorry. Only having a bit of fun.' He looked dejected.

'Well, if you want to join the gang then you need to play by the rules. Right, Tom?' Tank turned to his friend. There was no reaction, so he nudged him in the ribs.

'What?'

'Nothing.'

'I was just thinking,' said Tom, 'about that young lass you were out with last night. She was a pretty one. How did you come by her?'

'Oh, I don't know. She was just hanging around closing time

3

at the New Queen's Head, night before last. Why? You jealous or something?'

'No, but she did have such nice eyes, and I haven't seen hair as blond as that since our Sarah left home.' Tom wriggled about and ran an excited hand through his hair. 'So what did she let you do?' Samuel and Charlie looked up, their attention grabbed by the possibility of a dirty story. 'Come on, you must have tried something on the poor girl.'

Tank smirked. 'Well, maybe I did.' He paused. 'And maybe I didn't.' He turned away and chuckled to himself.

'Spit it out, Tankers.' Charlie had approached his friends and sat right next to Tank. Samuel followed suit and crouched low in the grass. Gabriel felt a warmth towards the lad who looked as if he were desperately trying to hide his curiosity and excitement at the prospect of the story.

'All right then, *I'll* spit it out. But I'm telling you *she* never did.' They all started to laugh. Samuel joined in, although he looked slightly unsure as to what Tank could possibly mean. 'Now, let me see, how did it all get started?'

Gabriel lay back in the gentle evening sun. The grass tickled his neck. He only had half an ear for the boys' conversation as he had heard these sorts of stories a thousand times before. They were funny and at times even arousing but he had other things on his mind. He never did understand why girls were so fascinating anyway. All the same there was something terribly thrilling about just watching the young men at peace by the river. Although he enjoyed it most when they took off their clothes and swam in the water.

He watched the lads' eager anticipation for Tank's tale. His gaze passed from one to the next, and before long came to rest on Samuel Grainger, who seemed different, more sensitive than the others. Gabriel studied the boy's dark, silky locks of hair, which flopped down over his eyes. There was something in his soft mouth and the faint growth of downy hair on the upper lip that pulled Gabriel in and made him stare, then shift his

attention downwards. Samuel had a strong, athletic figure, slim and tall, like that of a dancer, but he could see the beginnings of a man's muscles under his thin shirt. He smiled at the boy, but Samuel looked away in embarrassment. Gabriel did not understand why he was so drawn to the lad.

'What was her name?' Tom asked.

'Isabelle, I think. But to be honest I don't much remember, what with the drink and all that.' Tank closed his eyes for a second as if in careful thought as to the actual events of his night's adventure. 'It was not long before twelve by the time we reached the orchard at the back of Miltlyn Farm. You know, Mr Binding's place? It was such a bright night I had to be careful else somebody caught sight of us. Luckily there was nothing nor no one in sight.'

'Enough of the scenery, Tank, get on with the good bits.' Tom was obviously impatient and consequently a poor story-teller himself.

'All right. Hold your horses!' Tank drew in a deep breath and let it out slowly. There was no doubt, whether the tale was real or invented, the boy certainly knew how to keep his audience in suspense. 'Now then this Isabelle, or whatever her name was, says to me, "So, Alfred, now you've lured me all the way out here, what was you expecting to do with me?" And before she even finished what she had to say I'd grabbed her and kissed her right on the mouth, making sure I pushed my tongue inside and held it there. There was no fuss, so I thought my luck was in, and by goodness it was!

'Next I started to feel her tits. They were big and heavy and I could tell that the nipples were hard as iron. So, I slipped my hand down the top of her dress, got the pair out and licked the tips. She's loving all this. So I lie her down on the grass and begin to run my hands up her legs, see how far she'll let me go. "Alfred," she moans, "boy like you ought to know better than to be so forward. What would my father say?" I couldn't blinking give a sod what her old man'd make of it. None of his business.

5

'Anyway, I get to the tops of her stockings, and the ends of my fingers come to rest on her panties. By this point I'm rock hard, if you get what I mean.'

Gabriel wondered whether the boys did get what he meant. He was beginning to feel a stirring in his trousers, the start of an erection, even though he did not know exactly what it was about the story that thrilled him so.

'Kissing her all over, both tits bobbing about in my face, licking the nipples like there was no tomorrow, I started to slip a hand under the crotch of those little panties. Moaning and wriggling all over the place was Isabelle by now, knowing exactly what she was going to get. My hand was right inside her knickers and I could feel the hairs and soft bits that she keeps in there. I tug them down to her ankles. What a sight! If you could have been there and seen what she looked like, skirt hitched up, legs parted, the lot.' Tank paused at this point, as if to allow the boys to take in the story so far; a time for thought before the real action started.

Tom lay back on the riverbank and put a hand behind his neck to act as a pillow. With the other Gabriel noticed him touching his groin, straightening out the rumpled cotton trousers around a clearly visible erection. Charlie and Samuel looked on, both pairs of eyes fixed on their friend's bulging crotch. They too had a stiffness at the front of their breeches, probably aroused by Tank's story, and the thought of him, just nineteen years old and so rampant with girls. Gabriel stroked his hard penis through the thick material and wished he were in private so that he might be able to relieve himself.

'And then?' Tom demanded in an impatient tone.

'Well, I take both my hands and part her legs as much as I could and start to slip a finger into that lovely wet cunt of hers. She's panting by now, so I put my all into it. In for a penny, in for a pound, that's what I say. I pull the ruby red lips open and lick up the juice that's slipping from them. I can't stop lapping away, like a puppy with a bowl of milk. She tastes so nice, and

the further I push my tongue in the more Isabelle gasps. All this while my fingers are working away up her, going in and out, making her wetter and wetter.

'Anyway, I need a little pleasure of my own by this point, so I unbutton my breeches and underpants, slip them down over my arse and let my cock free. It's as big and hard as it's going to get, and certainly enough to fill old Isabelle up good and proper. Feeling those big tits with both hands and sticking my tongue in her mouth to stop her moaning, I decide it's time to put my knob up her. So I shove it in, hard, right to the hilt. She draws in a breath and closes her eyes. I fuck away, pulling my cock fully out and then driving it back inside, with her hands gripping for dear life onto my arse, just to make sure that she gets a good helping!'

Gabriel continued to listen, by this point totally enthralled, as the lads all chuckled, just like dirty little schoolboys comparing the size of their penises. Samuel turned over and rested on his stomach, as if partly to conceal his excited bulge from the others, and partly so as to be able to rub himself gently on the grass below.

'So, you see, I'm fucking quite happily, getting ready to finish, when she stops me. "I'm worried about . . . well, you know . . . I'm too young to get myself in the club," says Isabelle. "You'll have to stop. It's not that I'm not enjoying myself, but Ma would kill me." So, thinking that was my lot I pulled my cock out and fell back onto the grass, while she put her knickers on. Then all of a sudden she turns to me and says, "Look, I'll suck it for you if you like. Davie Dubbins likes it when I do his."'

'The filthy little bugger. Well, he certainly kept that one to himself,' Tom interrupted.

'Shhh,' Samuel said, 'let him get on with the story. I want to know what Tankers said to that one. And, anyway, everyone knows about Davie-boy!' He smirked and returned his attention to Tank who took a short breath and continued.

'What do you think I said? No thank you, miss, I'm not that kind of boy? Fuck I did! So with a nod she slipped down to where my cock was straining away, stiff as a board. Wow, what a girl! I've never been sucked off like that before. She starts rubbing my balls and at the same time wanks the shaft of my cock. Then I can feel her mouth around the head and down the length, until all I can see is a mop of blond hair bobbing up and down on the end of my knob. All the while she's squeezing my balls and I can feel myself starting to come.'

'So, how did it feel?' asked Samuel. It looked as if he had been taking in every word of Tank's story, and gradually getting more and more overwrought. Perhaps he wanted to be part of the gang, fit in with the way things were in the village. There was something quite breathtaking about both Tank and Tom's strong bodies and keen smiles, both the boys now clearly stiff with sexual excitement, and perhaps Samuel saw this too.

'Fantastic. What do you think?' Tank replied sarcastically. 'She kept me on the brink of spunking for ages. Every time I thought I was there she stopped, let me relax and then continued. Finally she wetted a finger and shoved it up my arsehole, and that was it, I couldn't hold back any longer. I came and came – and she lapped it up, drunk down every last drop.'

Sam stretched out on the bank of the river and stared at the sun which lay low in the sky and at the dark water running past him like a long strip of blackened glass. The trees that lined the other bank were utterly still, registering the absence of any breeze. A little further up-river, set back in low bushes and tall grass, was the barn that Tom's gang used as their hide-out, meeting place and private den. Sam stared at the building curious as to what happened in there when the boys were alone. A low wooden door provided the entrance, but what was within was still a mystery. He had never dared to go inside for fear of chastisement.

8

Sam glanced over at Tom and Tank who were lying on their backs with both legs bent up, their stiff penises clearly visible to all. Charlie sat a little further away, nervously biting the skin around the edges of his nails. Sam looked across just in time to see Gabriel raise himself from the ground and approach them.

'I'm off,' he said. 'Rosie'll be waiting and I don't want to be late.'

'All right. But I bet you could have more fun with us than with that bit of fluff,' said Tom, shrugging his shoulders. 'But, of course, it's up to you.'

'Well, if it's all the same I'll be off. See you later.' Gabriel turned and headed off along the riverbank, over the bridge and away into the distance. The boys watched his figure recede.

'Oh, well, where were we?' Tom jogged his friend's shoulder and gave him a wink. Then, trying to conceal his movement, he rubbed his groin and gave a breathy sigh. 'So, Sam, do you want to hang around with us from now on? Do you want to be in the gang?'

Sam blushed at the question, but at the same time could not suppress a smile at the prospect of what might happen next. He sucked in a breath. 'Yes, of course I do.' He paused and looked into Tom's eyes, slightly baffled. 'Why?'

'Well,' Tom looked a little nervous too, as if he were unsure as to the consequences of his words, 'there's a few things you need to do beforehand. To prove you're worth it, I mean.'

'What kind of things?'

'Everyone has to do it,' Charlie broke in. Sam swallowed. The palms of his hands were damp and he rubbed them down the sides of his trousers.

'Look, do you want to be in the gang or not?' demanded Tank.

Sam nodded.

'Well, follow us into the barn and we'll show you what you have to do.'

Tom leant over and spoke close to Sam's ear. 'But just

9

remember, no more questions. Keep your mouth shut and do as you're told.' The three boys led the way across the thicket of grass and low bushes, through the barn door and into the darkness within. Sam tagged along behind, more worried now about the task he must perform.

The interior of the building was dark and smelt of rotting hay. There was a hazy light that filtered through the cracks and splits in the ageing framework of the barn. Tiny fragments of dust floated about, caught in the rays. Beams ran vertically and horizontally across the old place, supporting a once-thatched roof. At the far end a ladder led crookedly up towards a ledge that jutted out from halfway up the barn wall – a shelf big enough to comfortably sleep four or five people. The rest of the lower floor was littered with odds and ends of ancient furniture, abandoned tractor parts and an excess of hay, much of which had fallen out of the bails that it had once been crafted into. Almost exactly in the centre of the barn there stood a table, sturdy and old-fashioned, with carefully carved legs. Lying across the table were several pieces of rope and a rectangle of grey material.

'There are two stages, if you want to join our gang.' Tom picked up the piece of material.

'What are you going to do?' Sam asked.

'Shut up! Don't breathe a word. And afterwards you must never tell anybody what has happened. It's a very big secret. If someone finds out there'll be no gang to be a member of.' Tom took hold of Sam and turned him round to face the back wall. 'Now stand still and do exactly what I tell you to.' With a swift movement he tied the cloth around Sam's eyes and double-knotted it at the back.

'Now, kneel down.' Although he could now see nothing, Sam heard the instructions and dropped to the hard floor. There was silence for a moment and then Sam felt a hand behind his head pushing his face into what must be Tank's groin. The sound of the lad's excited breaths and the location

of Tom's voice earlier indicated that the figure before him could only be that of Tank. His groin felt warm and soft and the material had a boyish, musky smell about it. Sam could hear a noise like that of someone unfastening the top of his breeches. Sam kept completely still, terrified as to what he would have to do.

'Open your mouth, Sam.' He did as he was told and nervously parted his lips. Although he could see nothing but a dark outline, the smell of Tank's crotch made him shake with pleasure. Never had he expected to be allowed such intimate contact with the muscular young lad. Sam was helpless, and all he could do was inhale the aroma of what he imagined must be Tank's private parts. A hard shaft touched the tip of his nose. It had a fresh, clean smell of soap about it and seemed hugely long. Sam's own penis was rigid by now and leaking a steady trickle of pre-come.

He lunged forward and took the end of Tank's penis into his open mouth. Immediately he felt a hand once again shoving his head from behind, forcing him to swallow the rest of the length. He gagged, but had no choice other than to keep on sucking.

'That's it. Keep it nice and wet.' Tank breathed the words heavily and Sam felt him pull his cock out and then push it deeply back into his mouth.

Feeling brave, Sam gently reached up and grasped the testicles hanging in front of his chin. Immediately they tensed, the sack tightening around two large balls, and he was able to roll them about in his hand. They felt warm and hairy. Sam grew more confident, knowing that Tank would soon begin to spurt, and lapped eagerly at the thick, solid shaft before him. The head was throbbing and secreting a steady flow of sweet-tasting fluid from its opening. Sam lapped this up with great gusto; he loved the taste of another boy's pre-come.

'Go on, Tank, fill him up. Make him drink it all.' He could hear Tom cheering his friend on. Tank groaned and thrust his

penis further into Sam's mouth. It felt as if he would choke, and he put a hand to Tank's stomach as if to prevent the lad from shoving it too far down his throat.

Sam's thoughts flicked back to the time when he had last given a blow job. His cousin, two years older than he, had bribed him with the promise of sweets and cigarettes. He recalled just how the seed had tasted as it shot out of the tip and onto his face and lips. Sam had made out that he really didn't want to do it but all the while had secretly enjoyed himself. Now in the damp barn he could not disguise his delight at the task. He longed to feel Tank spunking into his mouth.

Tank let out a low grunt and held Sam's head tightly against his groin. The end of his penis swelled and hardened, and with a thrust and a strain, Sam felt a jet of thick, creamy semen shoot down the back of his throat. He gulped it down, sucking desperately on Tank's ejaculating cock, hoping that the come would never stop. The wetness of Sam's mouth and the way he stimulated the head of the prick with his tongue seemed to make the orgasm long and intense, and Tank came until there was nothing left but a thin, watery trickle as the penis slipped from Sam's mouth. He lapped up what droplets of semen were left on his lips and savoured the salty liquid in his mouth.

Tom chuckled to himself as he watched the blindfolded boy gasping for air, his mouth still dripping with Tank's semen. He looked so helpless and pathetic, ready to do anything in order to get into his gang. He watched as Tank fell back onto the pile of hay that lay behind him, exhausted and spent, his saliva-drenched cock still hanging out of the opening in his underwear.

'Charlie?' Tom demanded. 'Now it's your turn.' The boy looked shyly over at his pal. 'Sam still hasn't finished his test. We'll give him a run for his money, eh?' He let out a cheeky snigger and gestured at the blindfolded boy.

Charlie looked nervously around. 'Are you sure I have to? It's all right, I'm really not that bothered. I'll just watch you lot.'

'Oh no. We're all in the gang together. What's good enough for one's good enough for the rest.' And with that Tom took hold of Charlie's arm and led him to where Sam knelt. He stood the boy in position and from behind unbuttoned his trousers. He pulled them down until they hung around Charlie's knees. 'Leave it to me. You just stand there and I promise Sammy-boy will give you a nice time.' With that Tom slipped his fingers under the waistband of the boy's underpants and gradually eased them over his hardening penis which immediately sprang out.

'Mmm. That feels nice,' he said.

Tom masturbated Charlie, one hand stroking his balls, the other pulling the tight foreskin backwards and forwards across the smooth, seeping head of the boy's cock. 'That's it, just relax.' He held the base of Charlie's cock and directed it deeply into Sam's awaiting mouth. 'Here you go, Sam. Another one for you.'

While Charlie shoved his penis in and out of Sam's mouth, Tom rubbed his hands over the boy's exposed buttocks, letting them wander between his legs and caress the balls from underneath. He was positive that Charlie would collapse from the overpowering sensations that must be passing into the head of his prick and through his whole body.

Tom wanted to give Charlie a little extra stimulation and he confidently prised the lad's buttocks apart and felt his way towards his most intimate boyish spot. He wetted his index finger with saliva and pushed it right up the hole, frigging it about, while Charlie released moans of pleasure. He could feel the muscles clench and the warmth from inside as he heard the familiar pants of joy that always accompanied a boy's climax. Charlie was obviously shooting jets of semen into Sam's mouth. Tom squeezed the boy's balls, curious as to how they felt mid-ejaculation.

Tom tried to imagine what it must be like to drink down the hot, creamy fluid. He assumed Charlie's seed was warm and thick and salty, perhaps because it had been stored for so long in the lad's inexperienced balls, awaiting release.

Tom pulled his finger out and allowed Charlie to sink back down next to Tank, both the lads gasping with fatigue. Spunk trickled down the side of Sam's face, a spurt having missed his mouth in his eagerness to capture every drop, and hit him there. He wiped it away with his hand, then licked it off, as if to savour the final reminder of Charlie's presence inside him. Tom felt a momentary jealousy at never having been in that situation himself, but the thought was quickly dismissed.

'You're good at this, Sam. Have you been practising?' He smirked and ruffled the boy's hair.

'No. I just –'

'Keep quiet. I'll do the talking around here, thank you.' Tom was feeling aroused. The bulge in his breeches showed a thick length of excited manhood. He was ready to take his own pleasure and at the same time teach Sam the most important lesson: who was master. 'Right! Tank, get the rope. Charlie, come over here. We're going to see whether little Sam's man enough.'

Tom led Sam, with little concern for the fact that the boy could see nothing, to the table in the centre of the barn and thrust him face-down. Tank approached, carrying two lengths of rope. He tossed one over to Charlie. The lads took hold of one of Sam's arms each and began to secure them to the table legs with the rope, so that he was bent over the table, both hands tied firmly down the side.

'Ouch!' Sam groaned. 'That hurts. What are you going to do to me? I'm not sure whether I want to go through with this.' The boy whimpered, obviously terrified at what he suspected would happen next.

'I thought I told you to shut up.' Tom gestured to his pals to move aside. 'Do you want to be one of us or not?' Sam didn't

answer. Tom reached under the spread-eagled teenager and undid the buttons holding up his breeches and underwear and with one harsh jerk he had them down to the knees. Sam struggled to free himself from the bonds that held his hands fast and made him utterly disabled, and as he did so Tom ran his rough hands over the boy's exposed buttocks and down his inner thigh.

With his feet Tom pushed Sam's legs outwards, spreading them as wide as was possible, so he could gain total access to those concealed areas. He raised the boy's shirt tails to get a good view of his back and bum cheeks. They were hard and round, full and softly indented at either side. Tom grabbed and prised them apart revealing a hair-lined crack, leading to a small puckered arsehole. He then spat a pool of saliva into the palm of his hand, rubbed it over a finger and stuck it into Sam's anus. With the tip of his digit he lubricated the lad's inside and with the other hand wiped the remaining spittle over his stiffened cock, which he had released from his trousers. The thing twitched, thick and veined, its harsh purple head seeping a little pre-ejaculated fluid, which now mingled with the saliva, and glistening in the pale barn light.

Tom, holding apart Sam's buttocks and pinning his legs outwards as far as he could, pushed his trembling cock into the tight pink opening and watched it dilate and receive his member. Sam let out a gasp and dug his nails into the legs of the table. Tom imagined how uncomfortable it must feel with the full length of his penis sunk inside him.

'Aaah! Christ, I'm gonna fuck you so hard.' Tom jabbed in and out of the tight passage, occasionally slapping Sam's buttocks, the friction beginning to stimulate an orgasm deep at the pit of his balls. He moaned and thrust harder, ignoring Sam's whimpering pleas to be gentle, wanting to take full advantage of this opportunity.

Tom noticed, out of the corner of his eye, Charlie and Tank looking on, their mouths open with the shock and thrill of the

lying there, coming all over his stomach and a thick line of semen dripping down Tom's hand. Tom wondered to himself whether, no sooner than this was all over and Tank and Charlie were home, than they would take down their pants and wank themselves off to the thought of what they were now witnessing. Tom knew that he would.

Sam took short gasps of air as if to calm himself after what had just happened. Tom wiped his semen-covered hand down the side of his trousers and straightened his bulging breeches.

'Well, I suppose you're one of the gang now,' he said.

One

———

James closed his pad and gathered up the palette and water-colour paints from the grassy bank where he had been sitting. The day was still bright, not yet five o'clock. He was about to set off, with mother and home in mind, when his attention was suddenly grabbed and an uncontrollable urge to stare overtook him. The object of his interest was a small gang of young men, boys really. They were kicking a ball about, shouting, racing to reach it first, and as they did so, shoved and grappled one another. You could not call it a game of football, more like a group of cats in pursuit of the same mouse.

Captivated, James sat back down on the grass, still warm from the indent of his buttocks. He stared straight ahead at the boys, none of whom could be more than sixteen or seventeen. Ordinary lads, out on a Sunday afternoon, trying to forget they have to work first thing in the morning. James was transfixed.

They wore light cotton shirts, which flapped and became almost transparent in the breeze. On their lower half they had on shorts made of dark canvas, heavy in texture, yet pulled up high enough to reveal the tops of their furry legs. Every once

19

in a while it was possible to catch a glimpse of thigh or a hint of torso, harsh and muscular against the natural backdrop.

The youths flew at one another, laughing all the time, as if there could be no other thought in their heads apart from the here and now. James wondered whether he would be happier to live the working-class lifestyle, free from the worry of university, a good position in the city and doing what was expected. They seemed so much happier than his family or friends, all of whom were tied down by their so-called duties.

All of a sudden the ball shot out of their area of play and towards James. He immediately flinched, terrified that it would hit him and make him look foolish and pathetic. The ball sailed through the air, and without thinking, as if it were the only thing to do, he reached up and his hands stopped it mid-air. A moment of silence passed while the boys stared at James staring at them. Nobody moved.

In bewilderment one of the lads jogged towards their lost ball. He had dark, shortly cropped hair and eyes that pierced straight through you, cold and angry. His mouth was full, the dark, wet lips looking as if they were permanently pouting. James did not know what to do. He felt a sensation of overpowering excitement at the sight of the boy's bare legs. They seemed to get thicker and hairier towards the tops. He also marvelled at the youth's muscular arms: with the shirt-sleeves rolled back James could see how hard his biceps were.

'Can we have our ball back?' said the boy. 'If that's all right with you, of course,' he added sarcastically.

'I'm so sorry ... yes, certainly ... I hadn't rea ...' James stammered, lost for words in the presence of such youthful beauty. The boy just looked on, as if amused by James's uneasiness, and grinned. Silence, once again. The boy came closer, and now James could see more clearly the sweet perspiration dripping down his forehead and the damp patch at the front of his shorts.

'Sorry if we disturbed you,' the lad said, and reached forward,

taking the ball from James, brushing him lightly on the hand as he did so. James tingled inside. The boy turned with a teasing, lingering look and moved back to where his pals were waiting for him. James watched two firm, rounded buttocks move up and down as they retreated into the distance. Something stiffened in his trousers and James panted as though he had just run from one end of the park to the other.

'James, darling, do take some more potatoes. You've not enough on your plate to satisfy a sparrow,' his mother insisted.

'Oh, for heaven's sake, don't go on. I've told you, I'm simply not hungry.' James placed both knife and fork over an almost untouched meal and turned away from her.

'Are you listening to this, Reynard?'

His father looked up from his plate with an annoyed expression on his face. 'What's that?' he muttered in between mouthfuls.

'This is the second night in a row that James has lost his appetite.'

'Well? What do you expect me to do about it? I've got other matters on my mind.' His father paused. 'I mean, ever since that terrible matter concerning Baxter Radnor, it's been nothing but work, work . . .' He stopped himself mid-sentence. 'Anyway, what am I going on about? Don't be so fussing, silly woman. The boy's old enough to look after his own stomach. Let him be!'

James's mother fell silent. His father took a large slurp from his wine glass and James cringed with embarrassment at what he might say next.

'And what's more,' he continued with a cough, 'the boy's probably just nervous about Oxford and all that business. Aren't you, James? Goodness knows I was.'

'But, Reynard, my dear,' his mother continued before James had even taken in enough breath to present his point of view, 'you didn't get into Oxford.' She smiled sweetly at him, and he

21

sniffed irately and started back on his dinner. His mother, although meek to the point of insipidity, always had the final word.

The rest of the main course was eaten, or in James's case pushed around the plate, in silence. Even the dessert was consumed with little conversation, other than a comment or two from James's mother concerning poor Lady Brighston's failing health and other trivial news.

'Did I tell you, Reynard, that I received the most touching letter from my sister Cordelia this morning? After all she has to put up with — no husband, a selfish daughter, a son with no sense of moral duty or respect for his mother — it's a wonder she's not been driven mad by it all. I must take the time to write back. Such a shame we do not see one another more often.'

His father left the table as soon as he'd drained his wine glass, leaving James and his mother alone while the maid cleared away the dishes.

'Oh, leave those for the moment, Tilly. And pull the door to on your way out.'

'As you please, ma'am,' replied the servant girl, curtsying at the door, a half-empty tray of dirty dishes in her hands.

His mother moved over and sat next to James. There had been an air of tension between them ever since James had entered the final term of school and sat his Oxford entrance examinations. He knew that the pressure had been felt by all the family, with the possible exception of his father who seemed oblivious to everything apart from the rate of inflation and the Dawes Plan.

'Are you happy, darling?' James's mother looked touchingly concerned. James looked at her with a sceptical expression.

'I'm fine, Mother. I just want to relax while I still can and do my drawings and paintings. You know that's what I like doing.'

'I know, but perhaps you should try to read just a *few* of the

22

books on the list. Oxford is less than five months away.' She put an arm around her son's shoulder and squeezed him with an attempted affection.

'Will you stop reminding me! It's bad enough as it is.' James pushed her away in annoyance. 'You know how I feel about the subject. It wouldn't be so bad if I was to study the arts,' he said, 'or even English or the Classics. But *History*. How dull!'

'Oh, but, James, you know how proud you could make your father and me, don't you?'

'I don't care. All I ask is to be allowed to spend the summer doing the things I enjoy. Painting, drawing, appreciating nature. I could be involved in far worse things. Look at what they say about cousin Barnaby.'

'I'm sure I don't know *what* you're talking about.' She looked away, frustrated. There was obviously nothing more to be said on the subject. She stood up and headed towards the door. Just as she was about to disappear out of the room she paused and turned to face James once more. 'I don't know where you get this taste for such –' his mother searched for the appropriate phrase '– bohemian pursuits. But all I hope is that you grow out of it soon. It looks to be so *unhealthy* for a young man who ought to have the mind for a more ... manly vocation.' And with that she disappeared from view. James sat alone in the dining room, listening to the clock chime nine-thirty.

The following afternoon was lovely and sunny and James decided to leave the house. He closed the front door behind him, and made his way, with silent steps, to the front gate of his London home. The house stood at the end of a terrace made up entirely of tall and narrow, four-storey town houses all identical to the Cardells'. The shutters were open and from outside he could see the heavy satin curtains, hand-embroidered with a delicate peony and oak leaf pattern. The door had been painted, on the orders of his father, a brilliant blue, which

allowed the property to stand apart from the other houses on the square. Mayfair looked so bright and welcoming at this time of year. The roses bordering the square opposite the house were beginning to blossom, and everywhere was so brilliantly green – nothing faded or parched as in those long August days.

London felt heated and dazzling as James left Belmare Square and headed, notebook and pencils in hand, towards Rosendale Park, a favourite haunt of his. The light there seemed to have a perfect quality, able to lift the subject of a sketch or painting out of its context and onto the paper with such ease it seemed the place had been crafted by one of the Renaissance masters themselves. It was Saturday, and people hurried about their business, oblivious to James's meandering steps along the pavement: mothers and fathers surrounded by chattering off-spring, elderly ladies in twos and threes, muttering about the old days. Like the flight of a thousand flocks of birds they passed him indistinguishable from one another.

The park was busier than ever, people being tempted out of doors by the sun and the prospect of swimming in the lake and relaxing in the shaded undergrowth. James walked across the lawns and down the pathways, finally settling close to the water's edge in the shade of the sweeping, rustling willow trees. He began to sketch the watery scene before him, but soon grew tired and lay back on the grass, resting his eyes. James slipped into a daydream.

His thoughts drifted back to his schooldays, when he had entered the Upper Sixth and had for the first time a study room of his own and two fags to keep it clean. Cantwell and Matthews, fifteen and sixteen respectively, were both bright boys, new to the school and eager to show their enthusiasm. James had grown attached to them and won over their respect and trust. Matthews was his favourite – a tall lad for his age, with ash-blond hair, that parted at one side and fell across his eyes. He had a muscular torso, strong legs and small, hard nipples which contrasted sharply with his pale body.

At the weekends, after rugby practice, Matthews would visit James in his room and ask if there was anything he could be of help with. The boy would still be wearing his kit and often complain of tired or stiff muscles in his shoulders and back. James would eagerly offer to massage the tender area, helping Matthews to slip out of his rugger top and lay face down on the bed. The pleasure he gained as he worked his hands across the shoulders and down the length of the boy's back, lingering over the soft waist-line, made James feel odd and strangely rude. He loved to make Matthews squirm and flex each muscle as his touch travelled here and there over the lad's body.

They had grown very fond of one another. On Sundays, with the permission of Matthews' house master, they took strolls through the countryside together, often stopping off for tea and cakes at roadside cafés. James remembered, on one occasion, kissing Matthews' stomach better when it became pained with too much walking.

However, not all was informality. In James's house, study-holders, even those who were not prefects, had the power to cane their fags. They were encouraged to exercise the privilege from time to time. It happened that Matthews was called upon to attend James in his room for some minor house duty, but failed to appear. James was able to overlook this small disobedience. However, the same happened on the next occasion – Matthews did not come to the room. When the boy finally arrived he was shabbily dressed and impolite. James, hurt by his fag's lack of faith and respect, felt there was no alternative but to punish him.

Matthews was made to wait outside the door for an hour in order to consider his discourteous behaviour. Then, when James had thought the public school pre-caning torture had gone on long enough, he sent for him. Cane in hand he had the boy bend over a chair, took down his shorts and delivered three smart, whistling strokes across his bare buttocks – the maximum penalty . . .

'I thought I recognised you.' A voice echoed, faceless, through the pictures in James's daydream and he sat up. He felt flushed and embarrassed to have been caught while his mind was so far away, dwelling on such forbidden thoughts. 'Sorry, did I wake you?' He rubbed his eyes trying to focus on the figure hovering over him, blotting out the path of sunlight. Gradually a big smiling mouth emerged and two gleaming eyes. It was the boy whose ball had strayed into James's hands the previous afternoon.

'Oh, no, not at all. I was just resting, that's all.' James brushed off the blades of grass which had collected on his clothing while he was asleep. 'I didn't expect to see you again.' There was an awkward silence. Then James continued, 'So are you with your friends?'

'No. They've gone off to Southend for the day, but I didn't fancy it myself. I'm not very bothered really about the seaside.'

James squirmed on the grass, trying to get comfortable, feeling embarrassed and yet desperate for the boy to stay.

'Can I sit here?' asked the lad.

'Yes . . . uh, please do. I was only . . .' James breathed a silent sigh of relief, pleased not to have frightened his new companion off with his own nervousness.

The boy sat down next to James, almost too close. He wore the same thin cotton shirt as before, with sleeves rolled up to the elbow and the collar unbuttoned and falling open to reveal his pale, hairless chest. But instead of the thick, confining shorts of yesterday he had on a pair of light, white shorts that elegantly traced the contours of his thighs and waist.

James could not help but be distracted by the boy's lithe body and angelic face, and could not remember being so startled at another person's physical appearance. His daydream had acted as an aphrodisiac and he kept staring at the lad beside him. His face was lean and had a charming, relaxed look about it. The nose was turned up at the end, which seemed to compliment his harsh cheekbones and strong chin. The youth's

eyes were a deep shade of brown and his dark hair was closely cropped against his scalp.

'What's your name?' the boy asked, bringing James back to the present.

'My name? It's James. James Cardell.' He paused for a moment. 'And yours?'

'William,' the boy replied. 'I saw you drawing earlier. Can I have a look?'

'Oh, I'm sure you wouldn't want to.' William ignored him and reached out and took the paper. 'It's nothing terribly special, I'm afraid.'

'Don't be stupid. It looks very good to me.' He held the picture against the scene James had been drawing. 'That tree's been asking to be drawn all year, I swear on it!' They both laughed. James liked his new friend and started to feel relaxed in his company. The boys lay back, propped up on their elbows, enjoying the ever-increasing heat of the sun.

After a while William said, 'Do you only do scenery? I mean, do you ever draw people?'

'Well, yes, but I don't often get the chance to have somebody pose for me.'

'I'd do it.' The boy ran his fingers through his hair and looked away. 'If you wanted.'

'That would be excellent. If you didn't mind.' James became excited at the mere thought of drawing something real, alive, breathing, and so beautiful and young as William. He pictured an artist's attic studio, pale summer light drifting in through an open upper window, and the lad draped naked across a satin-covered sofa. The thrill of living an artist's life held James in its romantic grip. Why waste his talents on History when he felt such a strong calling towards painting and drawing?

'What do I have to do?' asked the boy.

James swallowed and took a deep breath before asking, 'Could you take off your shirt? If you don't mind of course.'

William paused for a moment and stared, a confused

27

expression occupying his face. James was instantly gripped by a terrible panic which made his stomach turn over and a sickness well up inside. Had he gone too far perhaps? James stammered out an explanation. 'Well, I mean you don't have to ... I'm not ... well, it's not important. It's just that ... I thought it would make for a more interesting picture, that's all.' He waited in terror for his friend's response.

William smiled. 'Of course I don't mind.' James exhaled a quiet sigh of relief.

The lad looked about, checking the surrounding area for people. No one seemed to have ventured this far along the lake's edge, their location being so secluded and removed from the main area of Rosendale. James watched in rapture as his newly found companion slipped one button after another out of its catch and the shirt fell open, just as if he were alone in his room and nobody was watching. William slid both arms out, set the garment down on the grass and lay back, looking confident of his own beauty and oblivious to James's eager glance.

The sunlight touched the lad's exposed body so that it appeared to shimmer with a golden glow. He was smooth and almost totally devoid of bodily hair, apart from the boyish fluff that covered his legs. James sketched with animated pencil strokes, feeling as if the tip of the pencil were exploring and intruding on William's most intimate places. This was so much more interesting, thought James, than painting trees and hills and lifeless things.

'So, what do you do with yourself? Are you on holiday from school already?' James innocently enquired.

'Holiday? School? Are you mad! I finished going to school three years ago. And as for holidays, well, I can't even remember the last time I had one.'

James felt foolish for thinking that all boys were as fortunate as himself. 'I'm sorry. I didn't think. I just assumed –'

'Don't worry about it. Some of us have to work for a living,

28

mate. I'm apprentice to a carpenter. Just like my dad and his dad. Well, you can guess the rest. Just following in the family tradition. Hard work, boring most of the time, but you've got to do something.'

James could not think of anything worse than having to look at planks of wood all day. Thank goodness he would never have to worry about it. He felt sorry for the lad though, and wanted to help him out, rescue him from the fatuous world of carpentry.

William looked thoughtful. 'I suppose I enjoy it really. I've got my mates and a bit of money. What more can I want?' James could have told him, but he wanted to remain friends with the boy. 'Anyway, what do you do? I take it you're not part of the working world yet?'

'Oh, I'm just about to go off to Oxford.' William looked confused. 'You know, to university.'

'Right. Looking forward to it? Better than hanging around here all year.'

'I suppose so. I'd rather be painting though. History is so terribly dull.' James stared at William's hard, purple nipples, trying to take his mind off the thought of Oxford.

The sketch began to take form. James etched the shape of his model's body, following the lines of the torso and waist, shading in the taut flesh of William's stomach. He stared in amazement at the soft tufts of hair that formed a path around the lad's navel and led down into his shorts and whatever was within. James did not dare to think about what William would look like completely naked, even this brief display was enough to make his underwear stick up, slippery and hot. He tried to conceal his excitement, not wanting to alarm his model.

James was pleased with his sketch. Basic but effective, he thought. Anyway, how could one trap such essential beauty armed only with pencil and paper?

'Can I see it?' asked William, still lying on the grass with both arms resting behind his head, leaving his upper chest and

armpits fully exposed. James shivered and eyed the drawing cautiously. He was afraid that there might be something in the picture that would reveal his deepest feelings.

'I suppose so. But it's not very good, I'm afraid.' He handed it to William.

'Oh, I wouldn't say that. I think it's pretty good. Well, for a first attempt.' He scratched his chest and rearranged his shorts. James was positive that he could see a bulge in William's shorts and he stared hard at the lad's groin area. 'What's the matter?' William asked in a soft voice.

'Nothing.' James gathered together all his courage and continued, 'I was just thinking how lovely you looked, that's all.'

'Oh, ta,' said the lad. 'That's nice of you.' James could not hold himself back any longer and he reached out towards William's stomach and ran his hand across the smooth flesh. The lad did not speak or move away. James let his hand remain there, carefully rubbing against William's tightly packed muscles which rippled slightly beneath the skin's surface.

James knew that the bulge in the youth's shorts was the beginning of an erection. He took this as a sign to continue caressing and he placed his other hand on one of William's nipples and gently pinched it until it stood up hard and cold. The lad gave a little sigh and let his head fall back onto the grass. James rubbed a bit harder and moved closer.

William was clearly making no protest against James's wandering hands, so he carefully slipped a couple of fingers under the waistband of the boy's shorts. He could feel a soft bed of pubic hair and the end of something warm and hard. He had not felt another boy's penis since he had been at school and it certainly felt lovely.

The lad let out a deep groan as James's fingers brushed the tip of his cock. He wriggled his hips a little as if to arouse interest in the area of his groin, and James let his hand slip completely down the lad's shorts and take hold of his stiff penis.

It felt hard and thick, and as he gripped his fingers tight around the shaft it quivered slightly.

James's own prick was as stiff as a board by this time and stuck up clearly visible in his trousers. He gently rubbed it against the side of the lad's leg.

James knew that it would not be enough just to hold William's cock; he wanted to see it. So carefully he slid down the lad's shorts. He was not wearing anything underneath them and the long, uncircumcised penis revealed itself. James let the lad's shorts rest just below his heavy balls, which looked tight and were shrouded in a mist of fine dark hairs.

With one hand still rubbing William's stomach he used the other to slowly manipulate the lad's tight foreskin. He gently pulled it back until he could see the bulging purple knob – the most sensitive part of a boy's penis. A droplet of clear, sticky fluid seeped from the opening at the head of the prick. James dipped a finger into the liquid and raised it to his lips. It tasted salty and creamy.

He looked over at William's face, hoping that he had not seen his shameful tasting of the lad's secret juices. But William was lying back with his eyes closed and James returned his attention to the lad's prick. He pulled the foreskin backwards and forwards over the slippery head and watched as the boy's body shook ever so slightly with sexual excitement and a grunt of pleasure was snorted out. The thick member felt lovely and helpless in his grasp and he could tell that it would not be long before William would no longer be able to suppress a climax.

The muscles in the lad's stomach hardened and James knew that the intense feeling of gently wanking the lad's cock shaft had become too much. All of a sudden William let out a gasp and a jet of creamy white semen shot out of the opening at the head of the penis and over his chest. It spurted out so violently and so far that James thought he must have been storing it up for weeks.

The final spurt shot out over James's hand and he heard

William panting with relief. He rubbed the tip of his fingers into the thick ejaculated liquid and once again placed them to his lips. The substance tasted lovely and warm – just how he imagined William must smell and taste when kissed in those intimate places.

Without a word the lad pulled up his shorts, wiped the semen from his chest and onto the grass and put his shirt back on. He sat up and looked at James. 'That really is pretty damn good,' he said. 'I'll do it again for you sometime.'

James was confused. 'What do you mean?'

'Pose,' said William.

'Oh, I see.' James grinned. And he watched as the lad began to walk away. James's heart sank for a moment. He had believed that by some strange twist of fate he would be able to take William home and keep him, like a plaything, for good.

'See you. Good luck with Oxford, if I don't see you before.' William raised a hand and disappeared into the distance.

'I hope I *will* see you before.' But he could no longer be heard. James sighed and turned to the only thing he had left of the boy – his drawing. It was a pale, empty reflection of the real thing.

Dusk had passed over the park before James realised what time it was and how late he would be for supper. He quickly packed his pencils back into their case, folded the paper and set out towards home.

James sat on the edge of his bed, playing with the tassels that dangled from the border of the cover. His mother had no idea what it felt like to be addicted to something, desperate to make that thing the centre of your life. Art was for James the escape from, and also the root into, reality.

'Isn't it time you thought a little more seriously about Oxford?' asked his mother. 'Perhaps we should go and visit your new rooms again.'

'No, thank you,' replied James.

'You know how proud your father and I are of your achievement. It's better than we could ever have hoped. Such a good scholarship, one of the best in your year at school.' His mother uncrossed her legs, rose and moved towards the window. She sat in the window-seat looking out over the back garden.

'I don't know what to think, darling. You know I only want what makes you happy. Just tell me and I'll make it happen. But you must promise to concentrate on the Oxford texts and your future, James. That's all I ask.'

'Well, actually, Mother, what would make me happy is *not* going to Oxford.' James slumped back on the bed, took a book from under the pillow and began to read.

His mother made a despairing gesture and turned back to the garden. Something seemed to seize her attention down below; abruptly she took hold of the window and yanked it upwards. 'Tilly! Tilly!' she yelled. 'Tilly, what are you doing, girl? I told you to empty the leftover tea onto the *petunias*, not the *begonias*. Why won't she listen!' She shut the window with a bang.

'Mother, I was just thinking. What would you say to me going away to the country for a couple of months? I could stay with Aunt Cordelia.'

'James.' She seemed shocked at the very idea, and yet at the same time a look of curiosity glimmered across her face. 'I'm not sure about that. It's such short notice. She may have other guests. She may not want . . . Anyway, you would never get into the Oxford frame of mind stuck out there in the middle of Kent. It may not be the best idea at a time like this.'

'But, Mama,' James's tone softened and he stood up to face his mother, 'it would be just the thing to clear my mind of all this art. I could spend a month or two just painting and walking, take a break after school, get away from the bustle of London. Oh, what do you say, Mother? Wouldn't it be a fine thing to do?'

'For *you* perhaps.' His mother fell silent. James waited in

horrible anticipation for her next words. 'It might not be such a bad idea.'

The corners of his mouth began to curl up into a smirk, and immediately the smirk became a full-blown grin. 'Mama, darling, I'm right, aren't I? It would be such a splendid idea. I'm so glad that –'

'Don't jump to any conclusions, James. I've promised nothing so far. But perhaps it's worth a word to your father.'

'Oh, do ask him. Plead with him, Mother. He'll listen to you.'

'Of course it really depends on Cordelia. It's her house now. We'd have to telegram straight away. And she's always poor at replying in a hurry. Even as a girl she never could get anything done on time. But that's all beside the point.' With that she rushed from the room and her footsteps could be heard clattering off down the hall and towards his father's study.

The curtains trembled delicately with the breeze from the half-open window. It was as if a small animal were pushing craftily from the other side, trying to sneak into the room. Two in the morning and James lay wide awake as if nothing but death could close his eyes. What would his father say? Would Aunt Cordelia allow him to stay? The questions built up like a wall across his pathway to freedom and escape from his parents. The things he had heard about his cousins and their adventures all sounded so magnificent and daring. For goodness' sake, he was eighteen years old and quite ready to look after himself.

He could barely remember what Barnaby and Julia looked like it had been so long since he had last seen them. James could recall spending an endless summer with them in the far-away world of his childhood. As for Leo, their little brother, he was only a baby when James had visited. But something happened – there was a row between his mother and her sister – they had left, and for a long time no one spoke of the Compton-Crofts. They had always seemed to James to be the

34

side of the family everyone disapproved of; their lifestyle was said to be extravagant and exotic. Aunt Cordelia had spent her youth in Paris and she never quite recovered from the bohemian café culture of the late nineteenth century – the Naughty Nineties and all that. Julia and Barnaby had been given free rein, they could come and go as they pleased, entertain whomever they cared to. James longed to be at Sunningdale, the family estate, right this moment. Freedom was the only thing that he could think of; any opportunity to escape from the constant moaning of his mother.

James shifted about in his narrow bed, trying to make himself comfortable, but there was nothing he could do to block out the memory of the boy in the park and the prospect of a summer of excitement in the country. He reached down below the covers and stroked his cock which twitched at the thought of what William had allowed him to do in the park. James could not resist reliving the experience in the privacy of his own bedroom and he pulled back the covers and slipped his pyjama bottoms off. The sheets felt smooth and exciting against his exposed buttocks and he rubbed his arse against the bed and gently caressed his cock. With his other hand James cupped his balls and squeezed them in his palm. A mixture of his touch and the cool air of the room made them tighten and clamp against the base of his prick. He remembered how William's stiff member had felt as he wanked the lad to climax and his own cock pointed upwards, as hard as a rock.

James stretched the foreskin back in order to reveal the shiny head and noticed the first droplet of pre-come glistening at the tip. He could not resist dipping his finger into it and placing the clear fluid to his lips. It tasted thick and slightly salty and put him in mind of the lad's semen he had dared to take a sample of as it flowed over his smooth bare chest. He pulled the skin backwards and forwards over the head of his prick and the friction between his movements and the steady trickle of fluid seeping from the head made James's balls ache.

Gripped by a momentary desire to further stimulate himself, James released his balls and wet one of his fingers with saliva. He parted his legs and raised his knees a little before slowly guiding the slippery finger into the pouting arsehole. It felt heavenly sliding inside him, and his prick twitched violently as the digit pressed hard against his prostate gland. James imagined that it was William inside him. He closed his eyes and pictured the lad's thick cock slipping up him and thrusting itself in and out of his tight virginal hole.

The sensation of his own finger sliding about inside him coupled with the rhythmic stroking of his cock made James yearn to spill his load. He could feel the semen welling up inside him and he thrust the digit in deeper. All of a sudden he realised that he could hold back no longer and a jet of spunk flooded out of the tip of his cock. The feeling was sensational and sent shudders through his whole body. All the time he was spending the image of William flashed through his mind. Soon there was a large pool of semen on his chest and stomach. So intense was his climax that the thick liquid shot out of his prick and across his hands and body. James felt drained and spent, his penis became soft once again and he lay still on the bed, panting and exhausted.

Two

James's mother dropped a lump of sugar into her Darjeeling and stirred slowly, all the while seeming to take the greatest pleasure in allowing the cube to dissolve. She took the spoon out, tapped it on the side of the blue-flowered, gold-rimmed cup and laid it delicately down in the saucer without so much as a tinkle.

James noticed that, as usual, his father was paying no attention to anything that went on at the table. His interest was totally wrapped up in *The Times*, the printed pages held less than an inch from his nose, like a gypsy studying tarot cards.

'Will you take another piece of toast, James?' his mother asked in a squeaky voice.

'No, thank you.' James slouched in his chair slurping orange juice. Tired and bored, he had planned to make an early start today. There was a football pitch and lake about three miles away that he'd been meaning to visit for some time. It might be the perfect opportunity to combine scenery with a little life study, James hoped.

'Where are you off to today? Rosendale? I know how much you like it there.'

'No,' he replied.

His mother stared hard at him, as if to say 'well, where then?' but James ignored her, and instead helped himself to another piece of toast and the financial section of the morning's newspaper. For a moment he tried to pretend he was taking interest in the state of the country's economy, but before long threw the paper back down on the table.

'Well, before you stomp off out of the house, I have a little news for you.' She paused, looking out of the window as if something of great import had seized her attention.

James refused to fall for her obvious bait. Every morning his mother had some piece of worthless information dressed up as scandal or surprise intended to lure a modicum of interest from him. 'Really?' James kept his voice steady and nonchalant.

She raised her eyebrows as if waiting for a polite enquiry. 'Aren't you in the least interested? Because I'm sure that if you knew what I do you'd be just a little curious.' James saw her smile and push a crumpled sheet of paper across the breakfast table. It was a telegram dated yesterday evening.

He folded it out and read out loud: 'Would be an absolute pleasure. Stop. Come as soon as he wants. Stop. Telegram before arriving. Stop. Barnaby will meet him at station. Stop. Love as ever. Stop. Cordelia.' He put down the piece of paper and looked up at his mother in amazement. 'What? Does it mean . . .?'

His mother nodded a positive response to the unfinished question. 'I hope we're going to see a smile on that miserable face of yours now. I'm tired of seeing you behave as you have of late. Of course it's your aunt you really have to thank.'

James jumped up from his seat, dodged the corner of the table and planted a big kiss on the side of his mother's face. 'I can't believe it! So I'm really going to the country for the summer?'

'Yes. It's there in black and white. You can go as soon as you please. But just remember that this is a holiday where

you can get all this drawing business out of your system and come back ready to start Oxford with a new attitude – a serious one.'

However, before his mother had said all she wanted to say, James had run from the room, banging the door behind him.

'What's all the noise about? I'm trying to read. Can't you see?' James's father mumbled into his paper, without even looking up.

'Nothing, dear. Just James getting a little overexcited. However, I think we're in for a month or two of peace, and not before time.'

James leant out of the train window and watched his mother dabbing a tear from the corner of her eye as the train heaved and puffed its way out of Victoria Station. He stood at the first-class carriage window and waved, a little sad to think of the comforts and familiarities of London being left behind.

'Do write to me, won't you, darling?' his mother shouted over the hiss of the engine.

'Of course I will, Mother.' James fell back into his seat and pulled up the window sash. The wheels clattered and scraped over the tracks and steam obscured his vision, as the train heaved out of the environs of the city and through endless suburbs.

The compartment was empty apart from an elderly couple in the opposite corner. The man read the morning's paper and the woman was poking about in her handbag. James stared out of the window as the steam from the engine cleared and the city had vanished. He was pleased, but at the same time felt a little nervous, this being the first time James had gone away alone. Certainly he'd left his mother many times in the past, having spent most of his childhood at boarding school, and had often been sent on school trips to the country and even to the Continent, but now he must fend alone. He was grown up and capable of taking care of himself. James felt a little proud of his

mother for realising this fact and trusting him to cope by himself.

The morning was mild and fresh, with just the hint of a moist breeze, and fine clouds were busy drifting through a pale-blue sky. As the train gathered speed James saw, for the first time that year, sheep grazing in a field, lambs still nestling near their mothers, even though the spring that brought them into the world seemed long past. One lamb in particular caught his eye – the black sheep of the family was the expression people used. The little thing stood out so clearly against its brothers and sisters that James felt sorry for it, and yet at the same time slightly thrilled that it should stand alone and unique and never know how different it must appear to the rest of the flock.

James remembered William, the beautiful boy who had allowed himself to be drawn and touched so intimately, and felt a sharp pang of tired regret. He would never be able to possess a lad like that; take him in his arms and stroke his thick, dark hair, as they lay in bed, William's head resting on James's chest. The mental picture made his cock arch upwards and stick out hard beneath his trousers. James pulled his jacket across his groin in order to hide his excitement from his elderly travelling companions. They surely could never understand how natural a feeling this was and how beautiful it would be to touch William in the most intimate of places. James rubbed his penis ever so gently under the folds of his jacket and longed to relieve the aching sensation that passed through his loins. Now, however, was clearly not the right moment.

The train clattered on through fields and pastures, woods and scrubland, stopping every now and again to collect passengers or deliver them to their destination. Places he had never heard of rolled by: Sittingbourne, Faversham, Adisham, Aylesham, Cranbrook. James tried to picture these remote sleepy villages, hidden away in the Kent countryside, and imagine how Rolvenden, his own destination, would compare to these. He prayed that the village might hold some secret excitement that,

now he was away from the careful eye of his parents, he may be able to explore as fully as was possible.

Barnaby Compton-Croft, James's cousin, would be waiting at the station to meet him. Everything had been arranged. James wondered what his cousin would be like; it had been many years since they had played together as children. He knew that Barnaby was three years older than himself, and thought how odd it would be to meet again now, both having grown into adults. He hoped they would get on as well as they had done all those years ago, but the stories he had heard his mother whisper to his father when they thought he had gone to bed made James fearful that things were not quite as they were ten years ago.

James glanced at his watch and noticed that a full two hours had passed as he sat in quiet contemplation, with only the scenery as company. It was now twenty-two minutes past eleven. The wheels of the train began to slow, the clicking of the tracks grew less frequent and the whine of the breaks signalled his arrival in Rolvenden. The sign at the station declared the fact in bold, black lettering. James rose and dragged down the two cases that held everything he would need for his country vacation from the overhead rack. He flung open the compartment door with a hard shove and stepped carefully onto the platform, lifting out his luggage after him. The station master blew his whistle and with a hiss of steam and the release of the breaks the train eased into motion and glided off down the tracks.

Rolvenden station was almost totally empty by the time James had arranged his cases and straightened his newly pressed suit. Apart from those who had alighted from the train making their way towards the exit, there was only the station master and a lone boy seated at the far end of the platform. The former was making himself comfortable in his office, picking up a newspaper and preparing for the long wait until the next train was due. More significantly there was no sign of his cousin.

James lifted up his cases and began to stroll along the platform, still a little shocked that there was no greeting party waiting for him. In order to reach the exit James had to pass the seated fellow. He felt awkward and clumsy in his formal suit and heavy shoes. His cheeks glowed red for a moment or two as he became aware that he was being closely scrutinised.

'You all right, sir?' The boy spoke in a rough country tone which made James start.

'Yes, thank you very much.' James was too nervous to even look at the person addressing him.

'You look like you need a hand, mister, with them there cases of yours.'

'No, it's fine. I'm sure I'll . . .'

'Look, it's no bother to me,' the lad interrupted, standing up and approaching James.

As he came closer James took a shy glance and caught his first real view of the boy. What he saw changed his mind. 'Well, if it wouldn't trouble you.' James took a deep breath. 'That's terribly kind.'

The lad grinned in a cheeky fashion. He looked to be about the same age as James and had dark, floppy hair that from time to time he pushed from his forehead. His eyes were shiny and deep, glinting as if in mischievous invitation. His delicate nose was slightly turned up at the tip, like that of a puppy, giving him the aspect of an innocent youth. The lad's cheekbones defined a strong jaw–line that led down to his most striking feature – the mouth. This captivated James instantly; its soft, thick lips, pink and wet, took one inside where the flesh was pale and moist. He was one of those lads whose mouth seemed to be always slightly open, even when not speaking. James thought him the most beautiful thing.

'Here, let me take it.' The boy took hold of one of James's cases, lightly brushing his hand as he did so, and without the least effort, hauled it from the ground. 'So where are you off to, sir?'

'Well, that's the problem really,' James stammered, aware how foolish he must seem to someone so calm and lovely. 'I don't know exactly. I was supposed to be met here, but it doesn't seem like there's anyone around.'

By now they were out in front of the station and at the end of a long hill that wound down towards some houses and a tiny pub. There was no one in sight. Trees and fields were the only other sights and there was the most desperate silence all around.

The lad seated himself on the ground, his back against the station wall and his legs bent up and parted. James was free to view the boy's bulging breeches and the seam of material that led down between his legs. He was momentarily transfixed by the thought of the lad's parted buttocks lying beneath the thick fabric, and stared down at the boy's open legs.

'Who was it you were meeting?' The lad gave a short, almost inaudible chuckle.

James refocused his attention on the lad's face and blushed a little at having lingered too long on his crotch. 'Oh, my cousin. I've come down here to spend the summer holidays.' He paused. 'I do hope they've remembered I'm coming.'

'I'm sure he'll be here soon.' The boy smiled in a friendly manner, which instantly put James at his ease. 'What's your name?'

'Cardell.' James laughed at his own silliness. 'It's James.'

The boy extended a hand and took James's. 'My name's Sam.' They shook hands and it flashed through James's mind that Sam's touch had lingered a little longer than was usual in such a formal greeting. 'So is this your first time in Rolvenden?'

'Yes. In fact it's the first time I've been away from home by myself. I'm looking forward to seeing my cousins and my aunt. I haven't seen them for over ten years.'

'Is that a fact?' Sam moved a little in order to find a more comfortable position and James felt an overpowering sensation of longing to possess his bright youthfulness. How he yearned for a lad of his own age. James imagined what Sam would look

43

like as he undressed for bed at night; how hard and muscled the boy's upper body must be and what prize was concealed in his underwear. Yet he also felt edgy and ashamed at having such improper thoughts. 'What's your cousin's name?' Sam enquired.

'Barnaby. Barnaby Compton-Croft.'

'Oh, yes, I know *him*.' As he spoke Sam revealed the slightest glint of a knowing smile that made James just a little curious as to what the joke was. 'Indeed. The Compton-Crofts and myself are well acquainted.' He let out a disrespectful laugh that made James just a touch annoyed.

'Why do you laugh? What's the matter with them?' James prickled with chagrin.

'No reason. No reason.' Sam's face became expressionless and he stared at James.

At that moment in the distance there could be heard a crunching of gravel under wheels, and it was clear that in the middle distance an automobile was approaching.

'This'll be him,' said Sam.

The automobile pulled up directly in front of James with a screech of brakes and a black cloud of oily smoke. A figure climbed down and approached the boys.

'You must be James,' Barnaby said in a low, dry voice. 'My oh my, how you've grown.' His glance travelled the full length of James's body and a grin flickered over his mouth as their eyes met.

James was rather startled by the man's impudence and stood there lost for words. 'Hello,' was all he managed to say.

Barnaby held out a limp hand. 'Barnaby Compton-Croft.'

James grasped the hand and shook it. 'Pleased to meet you.'

'Well, let's not be hanging around here, dear boy. It's a bit of a drive, I'm afraid, so the sooner we begin the sooner we'll be there.' He paused to sniff and glance about. 'Now, where are your belongings?' Barnaby stopped short as he spotted Sam, who remained seated behind them. They exchanged a glance

that left James bemused. Sam remained expressionless, but a sparkle lit up the corners of his cousin's eyes and encouraged a smirk to creep over his lips. 'Ah, Samuel, what a surprise.' He hesitated a moment and then continued, 'You'll give us a hand with these cases, won't you?'

'If you want, sir.' Sam stood up and lifted James's luggage onto the back seat of the motorcar.

Barnaby opened the passenger door. 'In you get, James.' James did as he was instructed to and climbed inside. Barnaby slammed the door shut and disappeared for a moment around the back of the vehicle. In the driver's mirror James watched his cousin whisper something into the lad's ear. Then the other door opened and the next thing James knew they were off down the road.

It was a long drive to Sunningdale and Barnaby remained silent for most of it. James was nervous and did not know what to say to his cousin. He thought how his driving companion had changed since their last meeting. If they had passed one another in the street he would not have recognised him. That skinny, pale-looking child had grown tall and elegant. There was a harsh expression of extreme concentration on his slender face. He was a good-looking man with a wild mop of wavy blond hair that fell gently across his eyes, giving him the air of a poet or artist of some kind. James had been instantly shocked by how tall he was and how small he felt in comparison.

'That was Samuel Grainger. He's a good lad.' Barnaby glanced across at his cousin and then back at the road ahead. 'I'm sure we'll be seeing more of him soon.'

The thought of this pleased James and he could not help but smile inwardly. Perhaps his cousin wasn't as severe as he appeared. 'I do hope so.' The words, intended only for himself, had slipped from his lips.

Barnaby did not seem in the least surprised by James's obvious interest in a lad of his own age. 'Mother tells me that you're here to do a little painting.'

'That's right. I'm sure there'll be plenty to paint out here.'

'Indeed yes. I think it's a very healthy interest for a boy –' he corrected himself '– young man such as yourself to have.'

The scenery flew past as they sped down the narrow lanes, through the village itself and out into the open countryside. James's breath was taken away by the wind hitting him through the open window and the beauty of the early afternoon light. A sensation of utter tranquillity and stillness drifted over him. They drove on towards Sunningdale in silence.

From his second-floor bedroom window James had an impressive view of Sunningdale's gardens. They stretched away into the twilight horizon where they became a thick copse. James was terribly excited at the prospect of exploring them in the morning. He had the freedom of the house and grounds to roam and paint in.

The room itself was brightly decorated and simply furnished – a single bed, a wardrobe, two chests of drawers and a small sofa – but the room was homely and clean. The wall opposite his bed had a large archway cut into it which allowed him to pass from his chamber into the next. This was Barnaby's bedroom. A heavy curtain divided the rooms. His aunt hoped there would be no problem in being lodged so close to his cousin.

Upon his arrival there that afternoon he had been surprised at the sheer size of the building. There were two entrances to the estate, the larger and more travelled led directly to the village and beyond that the station. They had, however, taken the back approach, which ran around the perimeter of Sunningdale and slipped in along the westerly edge of the wood that James now observed from his window. The path had not been mended in many years and the journey had been a little rough. It was also impossible to gain a view of the house itself until one was directly upon it. James had felt astounded by the sheer size and stature of the building when at last it came into view.

The house had been built sometime in the mid-eighteenth century: a square Palladian building, four storeys high, with two huge wings either side that jutted forward from the main section. Fluted Corinthian columns supported the vast portico that drew the eye towards Sunningdale's total symmetry. The roof of the entrance was sloped into a triangle and a huge flight of stone steps ran up towards the main doors.

The dinner gong sounded, and James, dressed in his evening clothes, made his way down the dark corridor that joined his bedroom to the main landing. The stairs curved around in a dramatic flourish and he was overcome with a sense of awe at the grandeur of the Compton-Crofts' country seat. The hall was lined with objets d'art, collected on the Compton-Crofts' many foreign excursions. Asian sculptures, African masks and exotic tapestries gave Sunningdale a Bohemian air. There were also ancient European canvases of unknown origin side by side with the work of the more modern English artists such as Dora Carrington and Vanessa Bell, and, most strikingly, Scott Tuke. His sensitive impressions of undressed boys made James twitch with excitement, and he longed to be able to stare at them for hours, and maybe one day paint like that himself. These treasures seemed to jar with the austere exterior of the house.

James made his towards the massive drawing-room doors. Before he could reach them they were flung open from the inside. He stepped into the vast purple and gold room.

'James, my dear, you do look fine. But there was no need to dress on our account. This house has no time for formalities.' Lady Cordelia Compton-Croft, his mother's only sister, took his hand and led him into the throng.

James felt nervous and out of place. His life at home was certainly comfortable, but nothing compared to the luxury of his cousins' lifestyle.

'You'll remember Julia of course.' James took her hand and shook it lightly. She was a slender girl of seventeen, and James

could recall her vividly from his younger years when he would often spend time with the family.

'How do you do,' she said softly.

They had played together as children but neither then nor now could he gauge anything about her true self. Her face looked meek and pale, her long, delicate arms were bare and hung loosely at her sides, and she exuded an air of boredom.

'And this is Leo, your youngest cousin.' His aunt gestured towards a stocky adolescent, with cropped black hair that James did not remember. Leo did not speak, but simply gave a slight bow of the head. The boy must have been no more than thirteen and only a baby when James had seen him last.

'Barnaby – whom you've already met.' Standing close to the drinks table, sipping from a large tumbler, Barnaby looked sullen and disinterested in what his mother was saying. James attempted to catch his eye, but was unable to gain his attention.

'And lastly, please meet our other house guest this summer, Professor Albemarle.' James shook hands with a kindly looking middle-aged gentleman, who politely asked how James found Rolvenden and wished him a pleasant stay.

'Now, James, will you take a cocktail before dinner? Or perhaps you're a whisky man?'

James had never been offered alcohol in such a relaxed manner before and was determined to make the most of it. 'I'll have a gin cocktail if I may,' James replied nervously, hoping that this was the correct response.

'Barnaby, be a dear and get your cousin a drink.'

Barnaby did not reply or move, but took another slurp of his drink and sucked on his cigarette. His thoughts were noticeably elsewhere.

'Barnaby. Did you not hear me?' Lady Cordelia looked a little put out.

'Yes. I heard you.' As he poured the gin and martini he continued in a low voice, 'I won't be staying for dinner tonight, Cordelia, darling. I'm off out.' He threw a lump of ice into the

glass. 'In fact I really ought to be gone, so I'll see you all tomorrow.' And with that he passed the drink to James and headed for the door.

'Oh, darling, we've got guests. You're really very rude and ungrateful.' But Barnaby had opened the door and was out into the hall before she had time to finish. Lady Cordelia opened the door after him and yelled, 'What on earth will your cousin and the professor make of us, if you go on like this every night?' She glanced back over her shoulder at James. 'I'm so sorry, he's never usually *this* bad.' She put her head back out into the hallway. 'And don't call me Cordelia.'

Dinner had passed uneventfully after Barnaby's bizarre departure. Lady Compton-Croft had been as hospitable and generous as his mother had led him to believe, and even Julia came to life a little before the evening was out. Afterwards they said their goodnights and headed off in separate directions. James, tired from his journey and all the excitement of meeting the family and being in a strange place, had gone straight to bed. Although exhausted he was too curious about matters to be able to sleep.

He was intrigued as to the explanation behind his cousin's odd behaviour that evening. What could he have been in such a hurry to get to? What could there possibly be to do in such a remote and isolated Kentish village?

Drifting away across his rural-bound train journey earlier that day, James' mind wandered back to his own home in smoky London and the boys from the poor neighbouring streets; how they would give any amount of whatever they could spare to be where James was now. They looked so beautiful and disinterested at play on the common or smoking behind the closed-down market stands. James longed so much to be allowed to draw and paint their bright, smiling faces once more. With his one true passion in mind, the passion that one can feel when attempting to capture the beauty of life itself, James's

thoughts took flight across the fields of Kent, where nature seemed so close at hand, towards the childhood time when he had stayed with his mother and father in a rented cottage on the coast. How simple it all had seemed then. But now, although he was no longer ten years old, and the sea far away, the pollen-laden air tonight transported him back to that innocent time.

As he lay still in the unfamiliar bed James became aroused at the thought of all the adventures he might have at Sunningdale. He imagined village boys swimming naked together in the river, at ease with one another's yearning adolescent desires, and meeting later in the intimacy of the woods to indulge cravings too shameful for the public eye. The neighbourhood men he had passed in Barnaby's car earlier that day now became lovers and seducers, willing to take James from this humid second-floor bedroom and off towards some moonlight adventure. How he would love to capture their bodies on canvas; use his skills to tempt them out of their clothing . . .

The warmth of his bedroom meant that, even with the shutters latched back against the brickwork and both windows ajar, bed-clothing was a hindrance to sleep. James unbuttoned the top of his pyjama jacket so as to appreciate the breeze coming into the room.

Rubbing a hand over his smooth, boyish chest he brought to mind the handsome young man he had encountered at the station. He recalled the tousled locks which fell over the lad's deeply set eyes, drawing one on towards full, red lips always seeming to be parted, wetly, as if in astonishment. James began to pull his own nipples, rubbing them roughly between thumb and forefinger as they hardened and sent a shuddering sensation down into his groin. In his mind the boy from the station was allowing James to slip his breeches and undergarments down and caress his exposed cock and balls. James could just picture the lad's thick member hardening in his hands, just as William's had.

James's penis stiffened, his balls became tight and the cotton of his pyjamas stretched around the excited bulge. Hoping that everybody in the house was asleep, he withdrew his own aching prick. He slid the pyjama bottoms down below his tensed thighs, and cupped his testicles, massaging them in the palm of his hand. James remembered the station boy's heavy, round buttocks clearly visible through tight breeches, and tingled all over with excitement. Carefully he began to manipulate the foreskin backwards and forwards over the firm purple head of his cock, which now glistened with pre-ejaculated cream. His balls ached increasingly with each masturbatory movement. The station boy, he fantasised, was now bending over, breeches down, to expose a tight pink opening bordered with fine dark hair. How he longed to lick that precious spot, push his tongue inside, taste the lad's sweat. He clasped his testicles harder and wanked more rapidly as the aching feeling grew more intense.

James could feel the semen pushing itself upwards from the base of himself. It did not take much to make him come. His thoughts again drifted to one of his favourite wank fantasies, to the dormitory of his old boarding school, still fresh in the teenager's memory. He was in the showers after rugby practice, and there was Freddy Jameson's soft, wet body welcoming his touch. He could still picture the dazed expression on Freddy's face as the boy squirted out his semen all over James's hands and stomach, and the sweet taste . . . He licked his fingers now, tasting his own fluids, sticky and clear, and slightly salty. James wished he was able to suck himself off – swallow his own spunk – like he had Freddy's and the other boys', when they let him.

Suddenly there came a hollow sound from outside of the room. James started, and instantly the groaning feeling at the base of his penis subsided, and, with guilty alarm at the thought of discovery, his desperate desire to spurt vanished. Panicked by the possibility of detection by a member of the household, especially by his aunt, James pulled his night attire up around his waist and sat up in bed, holding his breath. Another noise,

much the same as the first, echoed through the room, yet this time James could almost make it out to be a groan. A groan, the sound of a closing door and a movement of bedcovers. Pulling himself over to the edge of the bed, a third sound told James that the disturbance had come from Barnaby's room, the room beyond the curtain.

James raised himself from the bed and crept towards the dividing drape. Pausing for a moment, not daring to be so bold, he breathed steadily and deeply, as silent as was possible. As James moved his ear in the general direction of his cousin's apartment there was a sudden, inexplicable silence. Perhaps I imagined it, thought James. But as he turned to move back to the bed a clearly audible sigh was released, the tone and pitch of which were not Barnaby's. Induced by curiosity he pulled back the curtain just an inch, enough to witness the spectacle within.

Barnaby was kneeling at the side of his bed sucking on the cock of a semi-naked boy. At first James did not recognise the lad, but when he looked more carefully he realised that it was Samuel Grainger, the boy from the station, who, with legs parted to allow Barnaby full access, was reclining over the sheets. His breeches had been lowered and lay loosely around his ankles. Barnaby paused for a moment in order to pull the boy's shirt open, wrenching at the buttons until they gave, and slid a hand across the muscular chest. He paused in order to lap at the tight stomach muscles that lay just above his soft pubic hair.

James was horrified, but at the same time so aroused that his own cock immediately sprang up once more, erect and twitching. He grabbed hold of it and tugged hard – an instantaneous reflex action. It was almost as if he were there, inhaling those enticing genitals.

Barnaby, unaware of his voyeuristic cousin, continued to explore his playmate's parts. He took the lad's penis deeply into his mouth, sucking slowly up and down the thick shaft, using

his hand to caress the heavy testicles. Barnaby's mouth was filled to capacity and with every suck there came also a moan of pleasure. With the other hand he gently inserted first one and then, driven on by moans of pleasure from the sucked youth, a second finger into the tight anal passage. The saliva that ran down from Barnaby's lapping mouth was enough to fuel the introduction of his fingers. James could see clearly the ecstasy on the boy's face – the feeling one only gets when on the brink of orgasm – and also Barnaby's desperation to complete his task, and so pumped his own penis more frantically.

The station boy arched his back, raising his buttocks from the bed, and drove his throbbing cock further into Barnaby's lapping mouth. James watched as his cousin slipped his fingers roughly in and out of the well-oiled interior. The lad panted with aggression, but remained poised, maintaining his masculinity while another boy performed such an intimate act.

'Aah, I'm coming!' he breathlessly yelped. Barnaby pulled the foreskin as far back as was possible and gulped madly as the boy began to spout hot come into his mouth and down the back of his throat. He pushed both fingers as far as they would go into his companion and twisted them to make the orgasm stronger. He greedily drank down as much semen as he could, but the station boy came and came, spunk squirting out from the tip of his penis, over Barnaby's lips and into his mouth.

Releasing his penis, Barnaby rose from his kneeling position and pulled himself up onto the bed. Lying next to the panting, spent station boy, he grabbed his hair and kissed him deeply on the mouth, letting hands roam over bare flesh, and semen seep from his lips and onto the boy's tongue.

'Sam, did that please you?' asked Barnaby, stroking his lover's face and lips. Sam nodded and put Barnaby's fingers, the ones that had been inside his anus just a moment before, into his mouth and tasted the aroma of himself.

'Oh, yes. Very much, sir,' he groaned in appreciation. 'It

made me feel lovely inside. Better than when the village girls make me spend.' He smiled in playful surrender.

'I'd like to turn you over now. Onto your front. And kiss you a little more –' he paused before adding in a whisper, '– intimately.' Barnaby placed the lightest kiss on Sam's lips as if to demonstrate. 'Would you let me do that?'

'If you want to, sir. But do be gentle. I'm not used to these sort of goings-on,' replied the lad.

James, still manipulating his own organ, could barely believe what was taking place. Never in a million years could he have anticipated an innocent trip to his aunt's turning into this licentious peep-show. Perhaps it was not right for him to watch his cousin's activities. Certainly Mother, if she found out, would never allow him to return, and probably not even communicate with the Compton-Crofts again. All the same, James longed to share this experience with someone. He held his body motionless for a moment, afraid that the boys would hear his sharp intakes of breath, as his own orgasm mounted inside him. Only in dreams had boys so freely allowed one another this type of bodily contact. How long he'd waited to see such a gentle demonstration of natural affection. If only he could capture this sexual freedom in a painting.

From his squatting position behind the curtain – reminiscent of Polonius spying on Gertrude and Hamlet from behind the arras, a play he had studied only the term before at school – James was able to pleasure himself while taking in the full spectacle. His virginal balls yearned to relieve themselves as he wanked his shaft. But not yet. The boys had not finished.

Barnaby lifted himself, still fully dressed, from the bed and began to disrobe. Sam lay silently, his once-erect penis returning to its flaccid state, watching his lover slowly slip out of the formalities of everyday living, pull free from his underwear, and watch the huge, stiffened member spring forth as if straining upwards to reach some unattainable heavenly goal.

Barnaby finished undressing and approached the bed, ruffling

the bangs of Samuel's hair. The lad remained still and calm, allowing his lover to remove the trousers from his ankles and also the shirt, open and clinging to his shoulders and back. He shut his eyes, letting Barnaby do as he wanted.

Kneeling over the boy's face, Barnaby presented his penis for inspection. Sam shuddered and reached out to stroke the tight furry balls and stiff length that twitched in his hands and released a clear sticky secretion from the penis's opening slit. He squeezed Barnaby's balls and lapped up the pre-come, taking in as much of the hard head as he could without choking. Barnaby snarled with pleasure, yet began to pull away.

'Not yet,' he instructed, withdrawing before Sam became too absorbed. 'I want to take a look at your bottom – acquaint myself with every part of you.'

Dismounting, Barnaby took hold of the lad's arms and turned him onto his front. He ran a hand along the length of the back – across the broad shoulders and down a clearly defined spine, like the indent of a fissure – ending just above Sam's taut buttocks. These, the highlight of his journey, Barnaby lingered over, marvelling at their plumpness and maturity, and at the same time their smooth, firm childlike quality. He moved both hands over the surface of the cheeks so as to detect the fine layer of baby fluff, pleasing to the touch.

Sam sighed and manoeuvred his lower half as if to invite further attention. Barnaby lowered himself to the floor close to the edge of the bed and positioned the boy's buttocks in line with his face. Then with a swift movement he grasped both of the supple globes and, parting them to reveal a thin line of downy hair along the crack between the buttocks, inserted a wet forefinger into the tight pink ring of Sam's arsehole. Sam took in a deep breath, and dug his hands into the bedclothes. Barnaby, almost shaking with anticipation, pushed in another finger and opened the anus a little more, placing his face close to the area in order to appreciate the faint, musty aroma – a delicate stench like stale flower-water or antique clothing – and

the beads of sweat along Sam's crack and perineum. Enflamed by the smell of the lad's most personal parts, Barnaby zealously tongued the exposed crevice, up and down across the soft hairs and deeply into the anus, pushing the lips outwards with probing fingers, his mouth enclosing the opening.

Sam trembled beneath, writhing with bliss at the tickling sensation of his seducer's slippery tongue entering him. 'Aah, that's so pleasing,' he murmured, angling his rear end as far into the air as he could, filling Barnaby's face, who now ate frantically, while grabbing hard at Sam's bollocks.

Not satiated yet, Barnaby stood up, thrust apart Sam's legs, and, wetting his own cock with saliva, directed the head into the moistened bumhole.

James watched in bewilderment, noting the look of biting discomfort on the station boy's face and his child-like whimper as Barnaby thrust his cock in to the hilt. He wailed in suffering, like a schoolboy being beaten by a master.

'Ooh, sir, that's so hard! You'll break me,' he cried, but Barnaby just smirked and lurched his cock unrelentingly in and out of the spread-eagled teenager, each withdrawal followed immediately by another violent thrust inwards, and the sound of a hoarse sigh, his balls bouncing against Sam's perineum.

Barnaby began to breathe even more heavily and all of a sudden stopped and let out a shuddering sigh, and, clasping Sam's buttocks, ejaculated. James watched his cousin shuddering and panting, and imagined the semen flooding through his cock and out of the tip, filling the lad with hot seed.

Barnaby pulled himself free of his lover and emptied the last of his sackful along the crack and massaged it in with the tip of his aching cock. His pleasure was complete.

By this point James too was nearing his climax. He wrapped his free hand tightly around the base of his testicles and pressed a finger against his prostate. With the other hand he frantically pulled the loose skin up and down over the now tingling, slippery head of his penis. He held his breath and froze. The

scene before him was enough to produce an enormous spurt of thick, creamy liquid that spattered forth and dripped down his half-exposed chest. The rest rushed over his hand and testicles, where James massaged it into the stretched skin. Spunk continued to run from the opening of his cock, and he licked some from his fingers. It felt rude and naughty, but tasted salty and pleasant. James exhaled as quietly as he could, not wanting to be detected by the young lovers.

'My word, you're a beautiful boy!' breathed Barnaby, once again licking at Samuel's anus, this time flavoured with his own emission. 'Mmm, you taste divine.'

'I'm glad to have pleased you, sir. We try our best!'

They moved together on the bed, Barnaby, still out of breath from the exhausting experience, running moist fingers through his village companion's hair. James watched them kiss deeply, then, cautiously allowing the curtain to divide their two rooms once more, slipped back into bed and closed his eyes.

Three

A knock on the door pulled James from his sleepy trance. He watched as a girl entered whom he'd never seen before and said something about it being terribly late and that breakfast was served. Before he could cross-examine her she was gone, the door once again firmly shut. James clambered from the unfamiliar bed. It was a bright Saturday morning, the sun streaming in through the unshuttered window, and James struggled with the sleeves of his dressing gown. He glanced down at his watch which was lying beside the bed. It read nearly nine o'clock. He had overslept.

James dashed into the bathroom, washed and dressed himself, then made straight for the breakfast room. It felt just like being back at school – never enough time to get ready in the mornings. He was breathless by the time he reached the bottom of the grand staircase and in such a panic not to be late for breakfast on his first morning at Sunningdale that he did not notice the figure coming towards him.

There was a crash of silverware and crockery hitting the hard polished marble floor, and the faint sound of an indignant curse.

'I'm terribly sorry . . . I really didn't see you coming. I was dashing to –'

'That's all right, sir.' A low country voice interrupted his apology. The redness that had flickered across his cheeks began to fade away and James glanced down to take a look at the face addressing him. Like a bolt of lightning illuminating the sky before one can even hear the thunder, so the face before him struck James instantaneously, deep inside, before he could rationally understand why. It was the most lovely and desirable face James thought he'd ever seen.

'Can I help you clear this up? I'm sure that it's the least I can do,' James offered in a desperate attempt to remain in the lad's company for as long as possible. Before him stood a youth of about the same height and build as James, who looked no more than nineteen or twenty years old. He had light brown hair, cropped closely at the sides and back, that drifted in waves across his forehead. His eyes were deep chestnut in hue, and his thick lips the colour of red wine. The lad's ears stuck out slightly, but this only made him appear more sweet and boyish to James. His face had an altogether childish quality about it, like that of a teenager on the brink of manhood. His body, however, contradicted that innocent visage with its muscled torso, thick legs and firm, rounded buttocks.

James studied the servant boy as he scrabbled about on the floor gathering together the knives and forks and shards of broken china. James was captivated by his guileless expression and watched him bending over and revealing the small of his back where his shirt had come untucked. There was a soft line of hair that led downwards to where the two fleshy globes met. James could feel his own cock twitch and grow hard in his trousers.

'What's your name?' In a moment of confidence James dared the question. What could this boy do anyway if he stared? He was surely only a servant, and James was a guest of the lady of the house.

'Gabriel Wood, sir,' replied the boy. 'I'm the odd job boy.'

James felt a little dizzy at the sound of the lad's rural tones pronouncing such a lovely name. Gabriel was surely the only boy in the world that James would ever really desire.

Barnaby perched on the edge of his seat at the breakfast table, looking tired and distant. James sat still and sipped his tea, not wanting to let his cousin know that he had been a witness to the goings-on of last night. And yet all the while he could not rid himself of a mental picture of Barnaby and Sam making love so openly and without the least care for the codes of the day. If only his life were a little more like his cousin's.

Julia and Leo had left the table and only Lady Compton-Croft remained to keep the boys company. James chatted politely to his aunt about the state of the country and what his father was doing. She was eager for James to experience as much of the country as he could in the short time he was with them, and to be as creative as possible now he was away from the watchful eye of her sister. The Compton-Crofts led a very different lifestyle to that of his parents.

'Barnaby is the perfect companion for you, James.' Lady Compton-Croft turned to her son. 'He shares your love of art. Don't you, dear?'

'Yes, Mother. It has been noted that I have an affinity with the higher levels of the contemporary visually-expressive media.' He crossed his legs and glanced across the table at James.

'Oh, Barny, must you always be so pompous?'

'I'm sure James knows what I'm talking about, Mother dearest. There are some things that only men can understand. You women are best suited to the domestic trivialities. We'll do the thinking.' He raised his teacup and shot a conspiratorial glance over at his cousin. 'Isn't that right, James?'

'Well, I suppose . . .' James could not complete his sentence for fear of looking foolish in front of his aunt. There was, however, something curiously arousing about his cousin's

behaviour and he longed to be given the chance to prove to Barnaby that he was one of the gang.

'Darling, must you be so rude to James? Look, you've embarrassed him.' Lady Compton-Croft smiled warmly at James as if in excuse for her son's imperious behaviour.

'Don't be a fool, Mother. He knows exactly what I'm talking about.' Barnaby winked an eye at James.

For a moment he wondered if Barnaby had known all along that someone had been watching his and Sam's sexual display. Perhaps he'd enjoyed James's roving eyes observing their shameful activity. There was something in that all-knowing wink that told James that there would be more fun and games to come.

There was a moment's silence which Barnaby broke with a gentle cough. 'Do you just paint still life, James, or does your interest stretch further than that?'

James was shocked at the question and thought carefully before replying. He didn't want his cousin to uncover his secret urges and lustful thoughts about the male body. But perhaps Barnaby was an ally and a confidant in these matters. 'Well, I'm not sure if I've really thought about it that much. I just know that I love drawing and painting.' James stopped to consider whether he should say what he wanted to say. 'Although it would be interesting and challenging,' he plucked up the courage, 'if I were to tackle the male form.' There was silence at the table. 'For example,' he added.

'Indeed, yes,' Barnaby said in a loud voice. 'Well, I'm sure you'll soon be able to.' He pulled his napkin from his lap and threw it onto the table. 'And now you must both excuse me.' He stood up and walked towards the door.

'But, Barnaby, where are you going?' James's aunt was distressed. 'I'd hoped you would be able to show James around the village. Take him down to the river. Show him the best sights to paint.'

'I'm sorry, Mother, but I really have to decline. As much as

I'd like to.' He shot an apologetic look at James. 'Ask one of the servants. How about Gabriel?' And with his words hanging in the air, he shut the door behind him.

'What a splendid idea,' Lady Compton-Croft exclaimed. James stifled a joyful yelp. 'I shall send for him at once.'

The two boys made their way down the back path and through the silent woods. It was a clear July morning. The only clouds in the pale blue sky looked like thin puffs of smoke and would soon disperse and allow the sun to break out. James, sketch-pad and pencils in hand, felt totally elated by the luck he was having: the splendid morning, the promise of a fine day ahead and the company of the most beautiful boy he had ever seen.

Rolvenden was a lovely, tranquil place and James felt certain that he would be able to paint well here. He adored the view, but not as much as he enjoyed Gabriel's company. He was certain that they would become the best of friends.

They passed through the village itself. Tiny thatched cottages and low stone barns lined the narrow lane that formed the town centre of Rolvenden. There was one shop that sold food, tobacco and newspapers, as well as serving as a post office and telegram bureau. Gabriel stopped here to buy cigarettes. Before putting one in his own mouth and lighting up he offered a cigarette to James, who declined. His mother did not think it a good idea to take up the habit, at least not until he was twenty-one.

'That's about it, sir.' Gabriel took a long suck on the cigarette and slowly exhaled into the morning air. 'Apart from the pub at the top of the hill.' They strolled in that direction.

'Please don't call me sir. My name's James.' As he spoke his mouth attempted a gentle smile.

'I don't know, sir. I'd feel a bit strange about that. The lady of the house wouldn't have it neither.' Gabriel's eyes lit up and the cigarette glowed in his mouth.

James looked longingly at his companion and wondered

whether there was any chance in the world that Gabriel might feel the same as him. Was the smile just out of pure friendship or was there something more affectionate behind those dark eyes? James felt helpless and ashamed at having such unhealthy thoughts.

The road took them past the public house and the railway station and out into the open countryside. It was not long before they reached a wooded area with a trickling stream that ran silently along the edge of the pathway. Ducks and swans travelled these waterways effortlessly and the water was clear enough to reveal the stony riverbed.

The path was overgrown and the boys had to tread carefully in order to avoid the thick brambles and thistles that slowed up their journey. Soon, however, James could see that they were reaching what looked to be a clearing. There was a stile which they climbed over and then a tiny bridge made of old railway sleepers. The river had twisted across their path and ran at right angles to its original course.

They were now standing at the edge of a heather-covered field, longer than it was wide, bordered at each end by woods and an old stone wall that ran the length of the field. This wall housed the remains of a once-impressive abbey. On the opposite side from this ruin there was the river, which now flowed wide and fast, its banks lined with delicate reeds and bulrushes.

The most striking feature of the area was the presence of a great barn which stood only feet away from the riverbank. Gabriel said it had been deserted for years and some of the village lads used it as their secret hide-out.

The boys walked in the direction of the barn, but as they approached they were halted by a rustling sound from within. This was followed by voices and the squeak of a door swinging open on rusted hinges. Three boys processed from the barn, laughing and chattering with one another. They stopped when they saw Gabriel and James. They were dressed in scruffy,

rural-looking clothes that were covered with dust and strands of hay. All three were in their late teens or early twenties, and had an untouched air to them.

'Oh, hello. Didn't see you there,' said the tallest of the three. James was curious as to the look of guilt and mild embarrassment on their faces as they left the barn.

'All right, Tom?' Gabriel looked pleased to see them. 'How are you all? Let me introduce you to Mr Cardell. He's a house guest up at Sunningdale.'

James blushed as he shook hands with the lads. He felt out of place with these working-class boys, he being the odd one out for once. He did not know their customs. A sheltered and privileged boarding-school upbringing did not prepare one for such situations. They all looked so young and energetic, and terribly handsome. He was especially taken by the two older boys, Tom and Tank. The younger lad, Charlie, was attractive but did not hold the same appeal as the others. James was puzzled as to what the boys might have been up to in the deserted barn. What could possibly have kept their attention and made them look so guilt-ridden?

'What are you boys up to then?' Gabriel vocalised James's unspoken curiosity.

'Oh, nothing much, Gabe. You know, just messing around,' Tank answered in an amused tone.

'Yeah, I can imagine.' Gabriel clearly knew something, which only made James more interested. He longed to get Gabriel alone so that he could quiz him about the lads' secret activities.

'We're going for a swim,' Tank continued, pointing in the direction of the river, which looked fresh and inviting. 'You coming in?'

'No. I think we'll pass on that one, boys.' Gabriel gestured at James to suggest that they move away along the riverbank. James was a little disappointed as he had wanted to watch the boys undress and dive into the water, but Gabriel put a hand

around his shoulders and guided him away from them. This in itself was enough to send a shiver of excitement through James's body – the boy he adored had his arm around him. 'Do you want to sit down for a bit?' Gabriel asked.

'Oh, yes. And this is a good place to stop.' They sank down on the grassy riverbank and made themselves comfortable. From where he sat James could still see the village boys, but no one would be able to hear their conversation.

James watched as Tom and Tank began to strip off their clothes. He could not take his eyes from the group as they pulled themselves free from the everyday formalities and stood on the bank in nothing but their underpants. Tom's lean torso and slender limbs contrasted sharply with his round, tight buttocks jutting out from behind. James was fascinated by Tom's finely muscled stomach and gentle upper arms, and especially by the inviting arse cheeks; the crack between them was clearly visible through his translucent cotton pants.

Tank was shorter and more stocky than his friend, but in his own way just as beautiful. A thin layer of puppy-fat still surrounded his chest, but it was clear to see the ridges of muscle forming below this outer boyishness: the features of a fully grown man straining to be released from the teenager's naive frame. As he eyed the boy James could make out a large, dark bulge at the front of Tank's sheer underpants. This made him stiff at the thought of the lad's huge cock beneath and what it must look and taste like.

The two boys dived into the river, followed by Charlie, more skinny and childlike in his awkward movements. They splashed about in the clear water, shrieking and shouting, and sending jets of water flying at one another. James looked on in amazement, thrilled at the sight of such titillating youthful activity.

'So, what is it that these boys get up to in that barn?' James asked in an innocent tone. 'They looked terribly guilty when they came out.' He let out an embarrassed laugh.

65

'Oh, it's not for someone of good breeding like you to know about.' Gabriel pulled a disapproving face. 'I can tell you that it's certainly nothing I have a part in.'

James's heart sank. 'Gabriel, for goodness' sake tell me what happens in the barn,' he insisted, staring hard at his companion.

Gabriel let out a sigh. 'Very well. But I don't know what the lady of the house – your aunt – would think of me saying such things.'

'Just tell me.'

'You see, the boys have their own gang. Tom and Tank are the leaders and that barn is their meeting place. They do with one another what men folks would usually only do with girls, if you get my meaning. Pleasuring each other.' Gabriel paused and his face glowed bright red. 'And if there's a new boy in town, well, they like to – what's the word for it?' He stopped in order to choose the correct phrase. '*Initiate* him.'

James tingled with excitement at the thought of those strong, manly lads taking pleasure from one another's bodies. 'Really?' he could not help exclaiming.

'Well, that's only what I've heard.' Although Gabriel seemed ashamed to have revealed the boys' secret club, there was an animated note in his voice. Could he be a part of the gang or maybe wish he was? James gazed intently into his eyes.

It was just after noon, the point of the day when the sun is highest in the sky, and it had become almost unbearably hot. The river shone like a mirror and the trees wilted under the sun's glaring rays. James had begun a simple sketch of the surroundings, positioning the river centrally as if he were viewing it from a boat. To one side he had drawn the trees and bushes that lay on the opposite bank of the river, and in the right-hand corner he dared a vague impression of Tank, Tom and Charlie. They splashed about in the water oblivious to James's artistic interpretation.

Gabriel rested while James sketched, lying back on the grass,

his legs spread out and crossed at the ankles. His eyes were closed. Every now and again James took a peak at his companion's ample bulge that showed up so obviously through his trousers. He was careful lest Gabriel should notice, and kept his glances to a minimum. It was pleasant just to sit there and draw and look at the boys.

It was not long, however, before James became bored with the scenery, pleasant as it was, and realised that to gain some experience of drawing the male body would be more profitable. The perfect model lay on the bank before him. He could feel a stirring in his groin as he summoned up the courage to address his companion.

'Gabriel.'

'Yes?' The boy opened his eyes and sat up.

'Gabriel, would you mind terribly if I did a sketch of you? You can say no if you like, but it would be such useful practice for me.' James held his breath.

Gabriel paused in thought before answering. 'Of course. Why should I mind, sir? It's not as if you want me to take off all my clothes or anything.' A broad smile lit up his face.

'Well, no,' James laughed nervously, 'but it might be a good idea if you slipped off your shirt.' Gabriel looked a little surprised and did not know how to respond. 'And after all it is very warm. It's not as if you'll catch cold or anything.' James had mastered the technique of enticing boys out of their clothing when he had met William in the park earlier that summer. He felt confident that Gabriel would comply.

'Very well, sir.' And without another moment's hesitation the lad unbuttoned the garment and slipped it from his shoulders. James could barely contain his sexual excitement. Gabriel had a slim but carefully defined upper body. There were no obvious muscles lining his stomach, and the smooth, taut skin looked soft and malleable. His pectoral muscles were subtly visible and capped with the most pert nipples, small and purple. The soft mid-day breeze made them hard. James was

surprised how pale Gabriel's body was, but then unlike his village friends who swam without shame or concern, and probably worked in the fields, his duties lay at Sunningdale. There would be little opportunity for him to gain a tan being inside the house most of the day.

James's favourite part of Gabriel's chest was the thin line of downy hair that ran from just above his navel and descended into his trousers. As he sketched and the boy reclined, James's eye was forever drawn back to that point where his chest ended and his breeches began. He yearned to be allowed the freedom to explore his companion's most private areas: to unbutton the breeches, slip them down and feast on the stiff member concealed within. James wondered what Gabriel's cock would taste and feel like as it glided over his lips and into his mouth.

As his drawing developed, so James's cock grew harder and he longed to relieve himself. The combination of the beautiful topless boy in front of him and the village lads swimming in the river made James quiver. As his pencil followed the lines of Gabriel's body, so it felt as if he were caressing the boy; intruding on his very essence. This titillated James, and yet at the same time frustrated him. He was powerless and denied the right to physically explore his model.

'What do you think?' James exclaimed, holding his sketch-pad out for Gabriel to view.

'Very good. It's a keen likeness, I must say.' The sparkle in his eye told James that his drawing was a success. 'Well, well, I never knew you were so good.'

'Oh, it's just a rough sketch. I'm sure if I had the time I'd be able to come up with something better.'

'Talking of having time, I'm afraid I will have to leave you, sir.' Gabriel was putting on his shirt and getting up from the bank.

James's face flooded with disappointment. 'Why?' he asked sadly.

'I have to meet my girl in five minutes.'

'Oh, I didn't realise that you had a girlfriend.' The sadness in James's voice served as the clearest indication of his distress. It was impossible to conceal it from Gabriel.

'Yeah, and I don't want to keep her waiting.' His face distorted into a shy grin. 'You know what women are like.'

'Yes,' James replied. But he didn't know what they were like at all, and was not about to find out now.

After supper James retired to his room and sat on the edge of his bed reading. The others were talking politics and the old days, matters that did not interest him. The day had been sunny and pleasant and he felt completely at ease in Rolvenden. He was pleased with his sketches, but every time he looked at the drawing of Gabriel, lying back in the grass, shirtless and relaxed, he felt an overwhelming sensation of unrequited lust and disappointment.

James tried to picture Gabriel and some girl together, but it only made him sad to think of him going to waste in the wrong arms. There surely could not be as much between them as James felt. Perhaps Gabriel was just deluding himself, trying to deny his true feelings, embarrassed at finding other boys attractive.

James lay back on his bed and debated what to do about this, and as he did so the curtain that divided his and his cousin's rooms parted and Barnaby entered.

'Hope I'm not disturbing you, James, but I thought we might take a walk together.'

James was shocked at Barnaby's dramatic entrance, and there was an oddly uncomfortable look in his eye that made James think that it might be to his advantage to do as his cousin suggested.

'I know it's late, but there's something I've arranged for you that I'm sure you're going to enjoy.' James opened his mouth to question Barnaby, but was silenced immediately. 'Don't say anything. Just get your paper and paints and follow me.'

'But, Barnaby, it's late at night,' James protested. 'Where can we possibly be off to?'

'Trust me and don't make any noise; we don't want my mother to hear.' He raised his eyebrows. 'We're going on a little artistic excursion.' Barnaby opened the bedroom door and marched off down the hallway. James, too curious not to follow, grabbed the tools of his trade and ran after him.

The boys slipped out of the servants' parlour door and through the herb garden, keeping close to the hedges, so as to avoid being spotted as they passed the drawing-room windows, where Lady Compton-Croft and her dinner guests were drinking cocktails.

James followed his cousin in silence across the lawn and towards the summer house that stood in a secluded rockery at the far end of Sunningdale's gardens. There was a glow of light from behind the curtained windows and James wondered exactly what might be waiting for them inside.

Barnaby paused just outside the door and studied his watch. 'Just in time.'

'In time for what?' James spoke abruptly, but his cousin gave no reply. 'And why do I need my paints. I'm not very interested in summer-house interiors,' he added sarcastically.

'Look here, James, my dear boy, sketching the view is all well and good, but there's more to art than still life. A lesson in the male form's what *you* need and I know just the boy to teach it!' And with that Barnaby turned the door handle and guided James into the dimly lit room. 'I should like to properly introduce you to a friend of mine – Samuel Grainger.'

James's heart pounded violently in astonishment. 'I think we've met before.' He held out a trembling hand. 'At the station.'

'That's right, sir.' Sam replied.

'Well, I'll leave you boys to get acquainted. And then you can get to work.'

'What do you mean?' James threw a startled glance at his cousin.

70

'I shall expect a splendid painting from this one, James. Models are hard to come by in this part of the country.' The door shut and Barnaby was gone.

'Oh.' James felt dazed and perplexed. He glanced around the summer house, not knowing what to say or do. The place was spartan and old-fashioned. A chaise-longue, two easy chairs and a low table were the sole items of furniture in the room. A standard gas lamp, which flickered and threw shadows onto the walls, acted as the only illumination. 'I'm a little lost for words, I'm afraid.'

'That's all right, sir. We can get straight down to it then.'

James reeled in astonishment, not knowing what the boy could possibly mean. 'Straight down to what?'

'The picture.' Sam seemed confused. 'Well, that's what we're here for, isn't it? Barnaby told me you needed a model. So, here I am.'

It all suddenly became clear to James. 'I see.' He looked down at the cold floor of the summer house and traced a crack in the stone with the tip of his shoe.

Sam continued to stare at him, expectantly. 'So shall I take my clothes off now?'

James gasped. 'What?'

'Or do you want to set up your things first?'

A momentary panic took hold of James and a thousand bizarre explanations flashed through his head. Was this a prank, a secret trick dreamt up by Barnaby and Sam to expose his true nature? Or could it be for real? There was only one way to find out, and what could he possibly have to lose anyway? If this was a cruel joke, he would call their bluff. 'No, you can go ahead, I'm ready.' James pulled one of the chairs towards the centre of the room and indicated that Sam should position himself just in front of the chaise-longue. He sat down and turned to a clean page in his sketch pad.

'As you wish, sir.' The boy took off his jacket and let it fall onto the seat behind him. Then bending over he unlaced his

71

boots and pulled them off, closely followed by his long, woollen socks. James could not believe his eyes. How long he had waited to see a boy so freely undress in front of him. He had the perfect model.

Sam showed no shame or fear as he unbuttoned his shirt and let it fall from his shoulders. The trousers came down next and were slung onto the couch. He stripped with a deliberate concentration, glancing up often as if to catch James's eye. It seemed like he was revelling in the idea of having a boy watch him undress and take pleasure in seeing his beautiful body revealed.

James's mouth became dry and his breath quickened as Sam neared the point where he would have to remove his tight cotton underpants. In James's trousers there was a swelling and a tingling feeling as the blood rushed into his cock and made it stiffen with excitement. He looked up and down the lad's smooth, pale body. His chest was lean and muscular, with large nipples that stood out erect. His legs were thick and covered with a fine layer of dark hairs, which became more dense as they neared the thighs.

Sam looked just as magnificent as he had done the previous night in his cousin's room. This time, however, James was even closer to the undressed boy, so close that he could almost reach out and touch the smooth flesh.

Sam hesitated and lightly touched the waistband of his underwear, beneath which James could easily make out the shape of his cock and balls. They were heavy and inviting.

'Shall I take these off, sir?' Sam's eyes were softly focused and he appeared to James as a resplendent child.

James did not reply at first – he was too amazed to say anything. This was such a beautiful moment and he wanted to cherish every second of it. When he did speak, he spoke with a quiet and nervous voice. 'Yes, please.'

With the greatest pleasure upon his face, Sam pulled his pants down and stepped out of them as they hit the floor. James

gasped slightly and could not help but fix his gaze on the lad's long, thick cock, hanging there limply, the foreskin pulled right down to conceal the glans within. And the heavy balls that lay behind, furry and tensed. James's own cock was now as stiff as it could be within his underwear. He moved a little in the seat in order to free it and allow it to rest comfortably. He feared that this was terribly obvious to his posing model.

'Is that all right, sir?' Sam asked. 'Is there somewhere you would like me to stand?'

'No. That's fine. Just stay there.' James could barely pronounce the words, so great was his sexual excitement at the naked lad before him. He turned his attention to the paper on his lap and began to pencil in the outline of Sam's body. He quickly drew in the limbs, his hands shaking as he did so.

When James arrived at the stomach and the groin, he paused nervously and stared at Sam's genitals. As he did so Sam's cock, in tiny, almost imperceptible jerks, began to harden and arch upwards. James could hardly believe what he saw. Sam stood before him, with a full erection. His balls were rigid and tight against the base of his penis. The foreskin had parted slightly at the head of his cock and James could see the pinkness beneath.

James looked down again and tried to sketch the boy's stiff member, but his hand trembled too much. Sam continued to pose, seeming oblivious to his erection sticking out in front. James felt embarrassed, and yet at the same time was filled with an uncontrollable desire to possess the lad as his cousin had done. A passionate strength flooded over James, and his fears subsided. He was a grown man now and capable of making love to a lad, just like a man does to a woman.

Overtaken with desire, James stood up and moved over to his model. He fell to his knees in front of the youth. Sam did not move away or even flinch. Out of control, James reached forward and touched the lad's balls; they were tight and slightly hairy. With the other hand he gently stroked Sam's stomach,

just above the base of his cock. Sam did not move away or push James's roving hand from him.

James took a deep breath and closed his eyes. He was unable to hold back any longer and slowly grasped his model's cock, pulled back the foreskin and let his lips circle the shiny, pink head that throbbed before him. Sam released a quiet sigh as James ran his tongue around the end of the shaft and up and down the length. One hand continued to caress Sam's balls, while the other roamed over his chest and thighs, occasionally resting at the base of his cock and at other times straying around the back and stroking the lad's firm, fleshy buttocks.

Sam's genitals smelt of lightly fragranced soap. They were clean and fresh with just the faintest hint of sweat, probably since they had been cooped up in his underwear all day. This, however, only added to their curious appeal.

James had amazed himself by being so bold and taking advantage of the lad's jutting erection. Sam neither rejected the advance nor reciprocated, but James continued to suck. He had now become more brave and allowed the penis to slide deep inside his mouth, the foreskin pulled back as far as it would go, and he squeezed hard on the boy's balls. James grew more excited, hardly believing what was happening, and sucked frantically on Sam's stiff knob, jerking the foreskin backwards and forwards in order to further pleasure the lad. His left hand gripped the boy's buttocks and at the tips of his fingers he felt the finest covering of hair just along the side of Sam's crack, the point where his arse cheeks curved together. James allowed his fingers to investigate the space between Sam's buttocks, and he slipped them down the crack. He ran them along the warm, moist pathway and they rested on the lad's tight, wrinkled anal entrance – the most intimate point.

James's prick ached and a trickle of sticky fluid moistened his trousers. He sucked at Sam's cock and lightly stroked his arsehole, as the lad's breath began to quicken and his stomach muscles tightened. James longed to swallow as much of the

lad's cock as he could, letting the penis slip in to the root and then out again in order to linger over the slippery head. Sam remained still, as if he were apart from the sexual antics taking place below him.

James could feel a trickle of salty fluid seeping from the tip of Sam's prick and he swallowed this with the greatest pleasure. Sam's whole body felt wonderful beneath his grip. He had the lad in his power, and he knew that sooner or later the pleasure of having his cock sucked would make him come. James could feel that moment fast approaching.

He dug his fingers hard between Sam's buttocks, but did not dare to insert them into the hole, for fear that he would pull away in annoyance. James sucked desperately as Sam neared his moment of ecstasy. He could feel a trembling tension in the boy's balls and the head of the penis seemed to get larger and harder than ever before. Sam let out a stifled gasp and James knew what to expect next. A long, spurt of thick semen rushed from the tip of the cock and into his mouth. How long James had imagined the taste of another boy's spunk, and now here it was running out into his mouth, warm and salty. He had total control over Sam's pleasure.

Sam's whole frame was tense as he ejaculated into James's mouth and trembled with the force of his orgasm. The semen flowed and flowed, at first in shooting spasms and then later in short trickles. The taste and texture of the come made James dizzy with desire. It was a lovely thought to know that he was tasting the beautiful boy's very essence; the most intimate taste of all.

The last drips of fluid were released and James let the boy's prick slide from his mouth. He gasped for a breath of air; every breath he had taken previously had been filled with the sweet smell of his partner's cock and balls. Sam remained standing, calm and relieved. He did not look down at James, and remained silent.

James's sexual appetite was even more potent than before

and the experience had given him the courage to go further. He longed to explore the boy's bottom in more detail. His fingers had found it pleasing, but they had had neither the time nor the courage to explore in detail. James summoned up the strength, and still in a kneeling position he turned Sam around so that his backside was now just in front of his face. The boy did not seem to object.

With care James stroked the soft, malleable cheeks that immediately tensed into hard muscle. They were coated with delicate, almost invisible hairs and stood at right angles to the tops of Sam's sturdy legs. The path between his buttocks was unexplored territory, and James's fingers trembled as they neared this lovely zone.

He took in a deep, sharp breath, laid one hand on Sam's back and guided the boy into a bending position. His arms hung limply in front of him, dangling towards the ground, as if he were about to receive a spanking. James's hard cock throbbed within his breeches as he took in the beauty of Sam's now semi-parted cheeks. He was, however, not as yet satisfied. He did not have complete, unobstructed access to the lad's most soft and intimate spot. So, with a gentle guiding motion, James pushed Sam's legs further apart, making him stand as widely and bent over as possible. He now had the lad's parted buttocks before him, and he paused before diving in to admire their smooth, youthful quality.

James felt terrified. He had never been allowed such free admission to another boy's private parts, and thus could barely believe that the opportunity had at last presented itself. He shook a little with fear and excitement, wanting to linger over the moment, savour it for later recollection, before his exploration began.

With great delicacy and tenderness James placed a hand on either cheek and separated them a fraction more; nothing was to impede his entry into the heavenly world of Sam's interior. James put his nose and mouth close to the crack and lightly

inhaled the boy's musky scent. His whole body tingled with pleasure at this arousing aroma, and he ran a finger along the soft, virtually hairless crevice in front of him. Sam's body tensed as the finger stroked his anal entrance and the hole tightened and expanded, like a mouth blowing a kiss.

James knew that this was the moment he had always been waiting for. He extended his tongue and licked Sam's crack. The experience was so intense that he licked again and again, trying to absorb the lad's secret taste. He now knew that he would be allowed to do as he wished with the body before him, so James pushed the tip of his tongue into the pink opening. Sam's arsehole dilated a little, allowing for further access to his interior, and he lapped at the muscled ring and the hard strip of flesh that connected Sam's arsehole and his balls.

Sam wriggled under James's grasp, pushing his arse hard into the boy's face, as if begging to be kissed more deeply. James needed no encouragement, however, and pushed his tongue as far into the boy's arsehole as was possible. He then gently inserted a forefinger, prising open the anus a little more, and slid his tongue even further inside.

Removing his face from Sam's arse, James allowed his fingers to explore the passage. With the lubrication of the saliva left from his deep kisses, he was able to introduce first one and then a second finger into the opening. James slipped them back and forth, probing deeply, feeling Sam's tight anal muscles contract and release their grasp. It felt profoundly intense, James thought, to have such intimate access to this handsome lad.

He withdrew his fingers and once again placed his mouth against Sam's crack and licked repeatedly, the mixture of his saliva and the lad's sweaty flavour mingling and making James frantic with passion. His digital examination of Sam's anal passage had opened the lad up a little more, and so this time he was able to probe even deeper with his tongue, the lips of Sam's ring becoming swollen and pink from James's exploration.

He withdrew his mouth, and as he did so caught sight of Sam's once again erect penis, jutting upwards from his pale, lithe body. His anal investigation had quite clearly excited the young man. Sam turned around.

'That felt nice, sir,' he said, looking James square in the eye. 'But now you've gone and got me all excited again.'

James was shocked, and yet at the same time pleased that Sam had broken the silence and actually acknowledged what had just taken place. He prickled with pleasure at the thought that the fun may not be over yet.

Sam leant forward, and to James's astonishment, planted a soft kiss on his lips. 'So what would you like to do now, sir?'

James was lost for words. Such a beautiful lad, all alone in his company, willing to continue these forbidden sexual antics. All his Christmases had surely come at once!

'Whatever you want to do,' James offered, quite unsure as to what would happen next.

Sam kissed him once more and then turned to where his shirt and jacket lay. He gathered them up and then spread them out on the patch of floor that lay between the two of them. 'Lie down,' Sam instructed in a kind voice.

James could do nothing but comply. His cock was as stiff as he had ever known it to be and he was totally overcome with desire. He lay down on his back. Sam knelt at his side and put his mouth over James's. His tongue slipped inside and their lips met and for the first time James tasted another boy's saliva. Sam's mouth was warm and wet, his breath had the fragrance that he had detected when standing beside so many of his school friends – boys he had never been allowed to touch or possess. They kissed for some time, quite lost in one another's mouth, tongues colliding and lips slipping about.

Sam's beautiful nakedness straddled James's fully clothed reclining body. He ran his hands along the line of buttons that held James's shirt in place around him and began to undo them. Nerves shook through James, as his shirt was slipped from his

shoulders and he felt Sam's hands travelling over his smooth torso. The boy began to delicately kiss his stomach and upper arms, his tongue and lips from time to time resting on his hardening nipples. James felt a tingling sensation like an electric shock run through his body.

Slowly Sam's attentions crept downwards. The tip of his tongue flicked in and out of James's navel and the lad's hands caressed his tightly muscled stomach. James could barely believe his companion's enthusiasm, his excitement at James's body. It was something he had been ashamed of before, not wishing to inflict the sight of it on others. But now another boy was finding as much fulfilment in his slender frame as he had found in theirs.

He held his breath as Sam unbuttoned the top of his trousers and tugged them down below his waist. He began to stroke James's inflated member through the thick fabric of his underwear, the shape of his cock and balls pressing themselves upwards, straining to be free. Slowly he brought his face close to the most sensitive area and lightly inhaled. Then he slid James's underpants down, and for the first time, clasped his penis with both hands and brought it to his lips. The sensation made James quiver, and it seemed like the feeling at the head of his penis could not grow any more intense.

Sam ran his tongue over the hard, purple head – the foreskin pulled back allowing for total access – lingering at the very tip, where a clear, sticky droplet of pre-come had oozed out. Sam greedily drank down the salty fluid, and his mouth enveloped James's long, slender prick. His hands found the tight, furry balls, and one squeezed them, while the other crept underneath, along the ridge of muscle that joins the base of the scrotum to the anal opening, and tickled James there. To accompany these movements Sam allowed James's cock to slip in and out of his mouth.

James could feel himself dissolve into this ultimate pleasure – the act he had for so long wished his school friends would

perform on him. He could feel the lad's hair flopping onto his stomach, and he glanced down to watch his head moving from side to side, the hair tickling him with every intake of his cock. James found himself drawing in breath with increasing regularity, and his mouth fell open in order to let out just the faintest sigh of gratification. The feeling of being on the edge of ejaculation engulfed his whole body, and the sudden introduction of a saliva-covered finger slipping with ease into his anus only served to edge him closer. Sam sucked with a frantic delight, as if he were trying to take in as much of the stiff cock as was physically possible. James gasped as the inevitable felt certain to happen at any moment. He placed a hand against Sam's forehead and pushed him away.

'Stop!' James panted, 'or else I'll spend in your mouth.' Sam paused and shot an innocent glance up at James.

'That's all right, sir. It's what I wanted you to do.'

'I didn't think you'd want to go *that* far.' A glint of excitement lit the corners of his eyes. Sam grinned in recognition of James's innocent surprise.

'I thought it was obvious from the start, sir, just how far I wanted to go.' He paused long enough for a smile to light up his eyes. 'When I saw you at the station I . . .' He stopped mid-sentence. Enough said.

The two boys smiled affectionately at one another, and James, his mind at ease and his confidence bolstered, moved his companion's head back down to its previous position. Sam re-inserted his probing finger and continued to suck.

Before long James was once again nearing his ultimate peak. He could feel the semen welling up inside himself: that aching sensation that he had felt so often when bringing himself off in the privacy of his bedroom, now he could share with another boy. So many times he had yearned to give his come to the beautiful lads he was never able to have, and now he was about to empty himself into Sam's eager young mouth.

He released a final drawn-out groan and then held his breath.

The spunk stored inside him rushed through his prick and spattered out into Sam's wet mouth. James could feel himself spurting jet after jet of hot, creamy fluid, the taste of which he knew well, that Sam seemed to allow to fill him. The finger in his anus pressed hard against his insides, increasing the orgasm's intensity, and for a moment he thought the feeling would never end.

James's semen now became a staggered trickle, but Sam still sucked furiously. His fingers were now entwined in Sam's hair, half pulling the boy from his throbbing penis as the sensation of his lips and tongue became almost unbearable, and half pushing him down on himself so as to fill Sam with the last traces of his come.

James was exhausted and drained. His whole body felt totally relaxed and he closed his eyes. As he did so he felt Sam move away from his cock, and a moment later appear close to his face. The lad's warm breath filled his nostrils and his thick lips were upon James's, and as they kissed, it was possible to taste his own semen still in Sam's mouth. It seemed all the more exciting to be able to take it from such a lovely youth's mouth.

'That was nice, sir,' Sam whispered. 'Did you enjoy it?'

James was almost too elated to answer. 'Oh, yes,' he managed.

'I bet it was a better suck than girls have ever given you.'

James nodded, not wanting to reveal that he was a virgin when it came to such things. He didn't want Sam to know how different he felt to others about girls. Surely this lad could give James far more than any female ever would.

'I must be going now, sir,' Sam spoke softly. 'It's late and my folks will be getting curious, what with me coming back so late last night. And now this.'

'Of course.' James let out a sad little sigh, but knew that it must be so.

Sam put his clothes back on and laced up his boots. James watched the boy cover up his beauty and wondered whether

he would ever have such an experience again. He slipped his own clothing back on, buttoned up his trousers, dusted down his shirt, and sat on the edge of one of the armchairs.

Sam hesitated in the doorway, seeming unsure of what he might say. 'I suppose I'll see you later, sir,' he murmured. The boys exchanged a coy smile and James watched the door close and Sam's footsteps echo away across the garden.

Four

———

It was a bright afternoon and James, armed with his usual set of pencils, paints and paper, cut a path through the woods behind Sunningdale. The sun was high and James's mind was full of thoughts about Sam and his cousin. He wondered whether he should say something to Barnaby, question him about the strange events of two nights ago. They had seen each other at breakfast that very morning, but it was almost as if nothing had happened.

James was extremely curious about the village and all of its bizarre goings-on. He was determined to understand what made the place so different from anywhere else he had ever been to. Although confused by Rolvenden's liberal atmosphere, deep down James was excited by all the possibilities that had suddenly appeared to him now London and his parents were far away. He felt liberated by having the chance to draw boys in the nude, and to have been allowed to go so far with Sam. This had fuelled his ever-increasing desire to do more of the same art. Barnaby was right: there *is* more to art than still life.

James followed the path as it wound through the countryside and eventually became the main village high road. He walked

through the centre, past the houses and the pub, and came out the other side, the side where the river flowed off into the meadows and then away to who-knows-where. The ruined abbey and the deserted barn by the river were his destination. That scene always drew him back. First, it was the loveliest and most picturesque part of Rolvenden, so secluded and silent. And second, it was where James had first been introduced by Gabriel – the memory of whom made him tingle with joy – to the village lads: Tank, Tom and Charlie.

James had thought often about Gabriel's words and his inhibited description of their activities. He could well imagine what the boy had meant by the phrase 'pleasuring each other', but he was still a little curious as to what had been intended by 'initiating' a new boy in town. James was scared by this possibility, and yet too curious to let the matter rest. He wondered whether he would count as a new boy in town; he was only a visitor and not of the same class as them. Perhaps it was an initiation reserved only for lads of a similar background, or a simple game that James had read too much into.

As he approached the clearing along the riverbank where the deserted barn stood, James hoped that the village boys would be there, messing about in the sunshine as they had done before. Upon his arrival, however, there was no sign of life. This gave James the perfect opportunity to investigate the barn, and he cut a path directly towards the old stone building. Before entering he put his ear up against the door and listened to find out whether anyone was inside. There was silence, so James pushed open the squeaky wooden door and slipped inside. It was deserted. Sunlight streamed in through the cracks in the ceiling and walls, making the straw that lay scattered in clumps across the floor glow. The only thing he could see in the place, apart from a few pieces of rusted farm equipment, was an old wooden table, that seemed strangely out of place in its rustic setting. The barn smelt homely and a warm, friendly atmosphere prevailed. There was nothing particularly exciting

or clandestine about it, and in the bright sun of a summer's afternoon nothing seemed sinister or secretive.

James left the barn and sat down on the riverbank. The grass was warm and the river drifted past as if it had nothing better to do than flow off into the distance. He unpacked his painting materials, and after deciding to make a rough sketch of the barn itself, began to draw in the outline of the building. As he did so there seemed to come from far off a sound of laughter and shouting. James could not decide from which direction the noise came, but as every second passed he grew more convinced of its existence, and more convinced that it was becoming louder and nearer.

Coming over the field were two figures. They looked young and male, and ran from time to time, punching one another as they went in a mocking way. They zigzagged their way through the grassy clearing and, it was now plain to tell, were heading towards James. As they came closer he recognised the two figures of Tom and Tank. James was both pleased and nervous at the sight of them. He had hoped that they would visit the river today.

They were both dressed similarly in coarse, heavy trousers, pulled right up over their thin cotton shirts and held in place with a thick, black belt. Their shirt-sleeves were rolled back revealing muscular forearms. The boots they wore were old and battered, the laces looking worn and barely holding together. They looked hot and tired after their boyish games and were slightly out of breath.

'Hello,' said Tom, the taller and leaner of the two.

'Hello,' James replied in a shy voice.

'Remember us?'

'Yes.' James was shocked at their audacity.

'What are you up to?' The boys moved closer to where James sat and glanced down to see what he was drawing.

'Oh, it's nothing. Just a sketch.' James blushed, embarrassed by people looking at his amateurish work.

Tom and Tank sat down on the bank either side of James. He felt surrounded and scrutinised by them, but it was, admittedly, at the same time, very erotic.

'So, you're staying up at Sunningdale?' Tank asked, his breath faintly detectable near James's cheek.

'That's right. With my aunt and my cousins. Just for the summer holidays.'

'So you're Barnaby's cousin?' Tom shot James an all-knowing smile.

'Yes.'

'Oh, we know Barnaby too.' He grinned across at his friend. 'We know him pretty well.' James was surprised that they should refer to his cousin by his Christian name, and wondered how it was that they knew him so well.

There was an awkward pause in which Tom and Tank glanced at one another and then back at James. Tank spoke first.

'So what have you been doing with your time down in Rolvenden? There's not much to do here. We end up having to make our own fun. Don't we, Tom?'

'Oh, I've been painting and drawing. That's what I like doing best of all.' The boys smirked at one another and James felt a little like the new boy at school, mocked by the others for not knowing the rules. But how could he know the rules if no one told him?

'So that was what you were up to with Gabe while we were swimming the other day.' Tom glared at James as if this was something to be ashamed about.

'Yes, Gabriel had allowed me to sketch him,' announced James proudly.

'With his shirt off?' Tom's comment immediately stifled the conversation, and James felt flustered, as if he had revealed the very essence of his desire for other boys' bodies.

'Talking of that,' Tank interjected, 'it's very hot today. I might take mine off.'

'Yeah, why not,' Tom agreed, and with a conspiratorial glance, the lads stripped off the cotton shirts and revealed their upper bodies. 'That's better.'

James was lost. Surrounded by their semi-nakedness, beautiful and dazzling, he felt shy and overdressed. It was as if they were doing it all on purpose, trying to test him in order to gauge his reaction to their care-free exposure. James was amazed at their loveliness. From far away along the bank he had tried to see as much of them as he could, for they had looked terribly beautiful even from that distance. However, from this close position they were even finer.

Both the boys' chests were smooth and subtly tanned from their constant exposure to the sun. They had a youthful, childlike quality to them, like the boys at school he had seen naked in the showers, that sharply contrasted against their emerging manliness. This manifested itself in the shape of hard areas of muscle, an angular shape to their torsos and the development of a delicate line of hair that ran down from their navels and into their trousers. James dared not imagine where it went next. Tom, however, was leaner and slimmer than his friend, devoid of the remaining puppy-fat that only added to Tank's boyish charm.

James blushed bright red and he felt his penis begin to rise and stiffen in his trousers. There was nothing he could do to stop himself. The sight of the lads' bodies was all too much for him. He was unable to conceal his obvious excitement from his companions, for there was nothing with which to cover the clearly visible bulge. His shirt was tucked in and he had left his jacket at home, due to the extreme heat of the afternoon.

'So, James,' Tom rubbed his smooth stomach and stared directly into his eyes, 'you don't mind if we call you James, do you?'

'No, not at all.' He could barely speak the words, so great was his sexual excitement.

'So, James, would you want to draw *our* bodies?'

'Well, I don't know,' James stammered, not quite sure what reaction was expected of him. 'It's all right, because I'm in the middle of another sketch, actually.'

'What's the matter? Our bodies not as good as Gabriel's?' Tom stared, anticipating a reply.

'No. They're lovely.' James instantly regretted his words, but had been unable to prevent them falling from his lips. 'I mean, they're fine,' he corrected himself.

The two lads grinned and James watched them look down at his crotch. They didn't seem at all surprised at the bulge in his trousers and said nothing. There was a moment of silence as Tom gathered his thoughts together before speaking.

'You seem pretty sound, James. A nice sort of lad.' Tom looked over at his friend. 'Don't you think so, Tank?'

'Oh, yes, very fair I'd say,' the lad replied.

'Perhaps you'd like to be in our gang.' There was a pause as James, shocked and confused, considered his answer; although it would be true to say he was not quite sure as to the exact meaning of the question. 'What do you say?' Tom prompted him.

'I don't know,' James stammered. 'What do you mean?'

'Well,' Tom scratched his chin, as if in careful thought, 'it means that you can hang around with us. Chat with us. Swim with us.' He stopped momentarily. '*Play* with us. You know, be one of the boys.'

James's heart pounded in his chest. What Tom was saying sounded appealing. He would do almost anything to be able to spend more time with them. They were truly lovely, and the sight of Tom's and Tank's tanned bodies was enough to make up his mind. James plucked up the courage and spoke. 'Yes. I'd like that.'

'Of course, before you can be a member we have to know that you like doing the same things as we do.' Tom paused in thought and rephrased his comment. 'Let's put it this way: there's a kind of initiation. Just to make sure we all have the same thoughts in mind.'

'What do I have to do?' James asked, his eyes wide with disbelief.

Tom looked across at his friend and nodded, as if to indicate that he should continue.

'Well,' Tank sucked in a deep breath, 'you know when there aren't any girls around, or none of the ones you know are willing to let you have your way . . .' He stopped to gauge James's reaction, unsure as to how his suggestion would be received. James's eyes lit up, now knowing exactly what the boys were hinting at. 'Us boys,' he continued, 'need to make our own fun. Take pleasure from one another.' There was an awkward pause as the lads stared intently at James, awaiting his reaction.

A smile lit the edges of James's lips. He could hardly believe his luck. What Gabriel had told him was true. They looked so manly and untouchable, and yet when left alone in each other's company had the same feelings as he did.

'So, what do you say?' Tom asked.

'Yes, I'd like to,' James replied. 'What do I have to do?'

The two boys led James into the empty barn and closed the door firmly behind them. They smirked and laughed together in conspiratorial glee, and yet at the same time seemed a little nervous, neither of them wanting to get caught or spoil the fun. Tom crossed over to one of the wooden pillars that supported the building and rested his back against it. He beckoned to James, who approached him nervously, unsure as to what would happen next.

'Right. Don't say anything. Just do as you're told and you'll be fine,' he announced in an authoritative tone. James nodded his head. 'Kneel down in front of me and put your hands behind your back.' James did as he was told. He watched, an anxious expression on his face, as Tom unbuttoned the top of his breeches and let them fall over his thighs. James could not help but notice the bulge in the lad's thin, white underwear. A thick rod, stiff and long, pushed its way through the material.

With one hand Tom pulled down his underwear so that it rested just below his tight balls. The lad's cock sprang out and quivered in the air in front of James's lips. He could feel Tom's other hand on the back of his head, guiding him towards the purpose of this initiation. James opened his mouth in readiness for the act he must perform, hesitant and slightly tense, yet full of excitement and desire at being allowed to suck Tom's beautiful prick.

James closed his eyes as Tom's penis entered his mouth, and his lips encircled the hard, purple head. The foreskin had not fully retracted, and he watched as Tom pulled the skin back, completely revealing the shiny head.

James kept his hands behind his back as he was told to, and sucked enthusiastically at Tom's cock. Tom thrust himself into James's mouth and used his hands to force him to take down as much cock as was physically possible. Every time Tom's body came close to his face, he could smell the lad's balls and crotch. The aroma of cheap carbolic soap, tinged with the musk of sweat, filled James's nostrils and he gulped at Tom's hard prick.

'That's it, James, get it nice and wet.' Tom made James swallow his full length, holding his head in place so that he could not object. He thrust forward so as to give James a mouthful, and Tank, who stood silently watching, a view. James loved having this strong lad's prick in his mouth. He could taste the steady trickle of pre-come that seeped out of the tip of the cock. Even though Tom was in complete control, James knew that it was only he who could bring the lad to his ultimate pleasure. The thought of having this power over Tom made him delirious and his head bobbed up and down in swift movements.

Tom released a soft moan, and James knew that the boy was nearing his climax. He could no longer restrain himself from breaking the rules and touching Tom. Without thinking twice James reached out and took the base of Tom's cock in his hand and began to wank him in the same rhythm as his sucking. His

other hand lightly cupped the boy's balls, and stroked their furriness. Tom did not object or move the roving hands away. He was too far gone. James sucked more frantically knowing that this was the moment he had been waiting for.

Tom let out an exhausted grunt and a jet of semen hit the back of James's throat. His penis quivered and the head became totally solid. Long spurts of come filled James's mouth and he drank down the salty liquid with great gusto, until the final drops seeped from the opening at the end of Tom's cock.

James relinquished his grasp and the lad's member slipped from his mouth. The taste of Tom's come was still with him, and he savoured its bitterness, licking his lips in order to soak up every last drop. James smelt his own hands, the ones that had grasped Tom's cock and balls, and the sweaty smell was still there – a reminder of the lad's body.

'Right. Your turn.' Tom motioned to Tank and then buttoned up his trousers, his penis still semi-erect. Tank placed himself against the same post and lit a cigarette. He unbuttoned his own trousers and pulled down his underwear. Having watched Tom's performance his cock was stiff and he was already very excited. James looked up at Tank's smug face, the cigarette pushed to the side of his mouth, and then back down at the boy's thick cock. Tank extended a hand and opened James's mouth by gripping onto his jaw. With his other hand he angled his prick into the opening.

James felt the lad's cock slipping over his lips and into the cavity of his mouth. Two boys, one after the other: James could barely believe his luck and gulped down Tank's cock. This penis was slightly different to the last. It was not quite so long, but thicker and firmer, the head more soft and sensitive. Tank smelled more fragrant and boyish than his friend.

Tom had taken some encouragement and manual stimulation to arrive at his orgasm, while Tank seemed, even at the start, on the brink of ejaculation. James marvelled at how easy it was to make the lad come. In a few deep movements of his mouth

and tongue Tank was breathing loudly and evenly. He could feel the lad thrusting forward, pushing his cock right inside James, on the brink of ejaculation.

With a shudder Tank squirted a warm, viscous jet of spunk out of his prick and into James. This first explosion was followed by five or six more, and then by a gentle trickle, as the final drops were squeezed from him and he fell out of James's mouth drained and panting. He fastened his breeches and stubbed his cigarette out on the barn floor.

Tom moved towards James. 'That was the easy part,' he said, rubbing his hands together. 'Now comes the hard bit.' James felt a shudder of panic run down his spine, and his stomach churned over. 'But as long as you do exactly what we say you'll be fine. Now, stand up.'

James was worried as to what exactly this second initiation could be. His curiosity, however, overcame his fear and he resigned himself to whatever it was that Tom wanted to do to him. The boys approached him and Tank began to remove his shirt and Tom his trousers. James remained calm and let their hands explore him. The lads undressed James slowly, inspecting his body at every point and gently rubbing his chest and legs.

Then James stood naked, apart from his cotton underpants which covered his aching erection. He felt ashamed and awkward. The boys still had their trousers and boots on – their shirts had been left outside – and he had hardly anything to hide his modesty. It was like being examined by the doctor when he was at school. He could remember having to strip naked in front of the medical officer, have his balls squeezed in a cold hand, his penis examined and a probing finger slip up his bottom. This was how he felt now.

'Right. Let's get these down and take a closer look at you,' Tom said, looking at the bulge in James's underpants. He squatted down in front of him and, slipping his fingers into the waistband of the underwear, pulled them right down to the ground. 'My, my, you are excited, Mr James, aren't you?'

James turned a brilliant shade of purple. He had never felt so embarrassed and exposed in all his life, but there was nothing he could do. Tom reached forward and grasped his cock. He tugged the foreskin back and exposed the pink, glistening head. At the same time he reached down and took a firm hold of James's balls, grinning cheekily and staring him straight in the eye. Tom, with a rough movement of his wrist, wanked James's cock, each time drawing the tight foreskin forward over the head and then tugging it right back again.

James dissolved with pleasure from Tom's jerking hand, and felt himself being drawn out. An aching at the base of his prick that had begun when he had first set eyes on the lads' bare chests, now erupted inside him, pushing its way into his balls and through his body. He could feel Tank's hands wandering over his back and exposed buttocks, venturing between the cheeks and stroking his inner thighs.

He felt as if he could hold back no longer, the groping hands of the lads was all too much, but he held his orgasm back, fighting violently against the desire to shoot off his semen. However, just at the moment when he thought he could restrain himself no longer, Tom stopped wanking him. It was almost as if the lad could tell, just from looking in his eyes, that he was about to come, and so, to tease and frustrate James even more, he had stopped.

'Did you like that?' Tom asked in a taunting voice. But James could not reply, he was too exhausted and panted loudly, both relieved that Tom's hands had relinquished their frantic grasp, and unfulfilled at not having reached his orgasm. 'Right, get on the table.' Tom gestured towards the table in the centre of the barn that James had noticed earlier in the day.

James, now completely naked, walked over and sat himself on the edge of the table. Tom moved across and stood directly in front of him. 'Lie back. And put your legs in the air,' he instructed, pushing James back as he did so. He lay there, fearful of what was about to happen, his hard-on still throbbing and

his legs parted and raised above him. Tom came in close and stood between his thighs. Tank approached at his left side and stood motionless, glancing at his friend, as if awaiting further orders.

James had a good idea what was going to happen next. He had thought about it so many times and had longed to know exactly what it would feel like to have another boy inside him. Now it was about to happen. Such beautiful lads, as well, he should not complain, but a sense of panic overtook him. 'I don't know whether I really want to . . .' he blurted out. 'I've never –'

Tom silenced him. 'Shut up.' He pointed an accusing finger at James and his voice grew louder. 'If you want to join in and be one of us then I advise you to shut your mouth.' Tom's tone became a little kinder. He did not want to frighten James off. 'We've all had to do it. It's part of the game. And anyway,' he continued, 'you might just enjoy yourself.' And with that Tom took from his pocket a small tin, that once would have contained snuff, and flipped open the lid. Inside there was a sticky substance, some kind of grease, which Tom took a scoop of on the tip of his forefinger. He parted James's legs as far as they would go, his knees bent up towards his stomach, and wiped some of the grease around his arsehole. It felt cold and slippery, and James winced slightly as two of Tom's fingers worked their way into him.

Many times in the past James had stimulated himself with his own fingers, but now he felt helpless and invaded as Tom took complete control of his body and slipped two slick digits in up to the knuckle. James felt overcome by this bizarre sensation, at once painful and uncomfortable, and yet almost overpoweringly delightful. Tom's intruding fingers, pressed hard against his prostate, made James's cock twitch with frustration. The feeling of the lad's strong grasp around his thigh and the jamming of his fingers into him made James shudder and wriggle as he lay there supine and helpless. His anal passage felt traversed and

slippery. James had been violated, but how lovely this violation was!

Tom withdrew his fingers and James gulped down a breath in shock. He could see Tom undoing his breeches once more, pulling them down and getting his cock out, which was now once more erect. He took up the container of grease that he had set to rest on the table and wiped some on his prick. James watched in trepidation as Tom pulled his foreskin back and rubbed the ointment over the head, so that it glistened like a soldier's shiny sword. And just like such a weapon it would soon pierce him, and tear away his virginity.

Tom once again wiped the remaining lubricant over James's tightly muscled hole. 'Right. Here we go,' Tom breathed, more to himself than anyone else. 'This won't hurt a bit.' He pushed his cock forward until it made contact with James's pink opening. James tried to breath in a steady fashion, remain calm, as he knew that the more tense he was the harder it would be for him. He could do nothing now but surrender himself up to Tom's aggressive desire to possess him. James felt the knob entering him and he let out a yelp, more in shock than pain. However, there was still a tremendous feeling of aching discomfort, and he had to restrain himself from yelling out loud. With another thrust half of Tom's prick had been rammed into him and, for the first time, he could feel his internal muscles relaxing around the thick intruder, gripping hold of the lad's member and accommodating it within him.

'Almost there,' Tom sighed and shoved the rest in. James groaned, the feeling of the lad's cock inside him utterly overwhelming, but gradually he loosened up and the pain became less. 'There you go.' James could not believe that the boy was completely inside him. He reached down, still not believing, and touched Tom's groin. It was true, he was all the way in him, right up to the hilt.

No sooner had he established the fact than Tom pushed his hand away and began to draw his cock out once more. He

withdrew it so far that James felt it would slide from him altogether. The feeling was sublime. However, as soon as he had once again relaxed into this new position, Tom forced his prick once more into James's anus. The whole cycle then took place again, and again, getting faster and more violent each time.

The lubrication Tom had provided allowed his cock to slide in and out easily, only hindered by James's tightness and inexperience. He became more at ease with the feeling, and the pleasure inherent in it soon overwhelmed him, each stroke of Tom's prick, thrusting deeply into his most intimate and least chartered zone, sending a thrill of indescribable delight shuddering through him.

He loved the feeling of this beautiful youth inside him. It made him writhe and pant, and his cock twitched in time to the rhythm of Tom's plunges. He longed to touch himself, wank his own shaft – just as Tom was using James's arsehole to wank his – and let the spunk spurt out in blissful release. Carefully he moved his hand down and touched the tip of his penis. A sticky stream of fluid had seeped out of the tip and onto his stomach and James dipped a finger into it. Immediately he did this Tank, who had been observing the whole initiation from the side of the table, slapped James's hand. He then looked towards Tom, who nodded, and he took hold of James's prick. His whole body shook with the thrill of the lad's touch.

Tank wet his hand with the pre-come and massaged it into the head of James's cock, stretching back the foreskin as he did so. He slowly jerked the skin back and forth while stroking his balls where they hung an inch above Tom's stabbing prick and James's stretched hole. James had never imagined such a pleasure as this; the stimulation from the penis inside him, jamming regularly against his prostate, combined with the aching inevitability of his ejaculation that Tank prompted with every movement of his wrist.

Tom continued to push his cock in and out of James,

regardless of whether it was hurting him or not. His eyes looked distant and he panted breathlessly. James was engulfed in his own pleasure and felt that if Tank did not refrain from masturbating him, he too would soon come.

Tom's movements became frantic and he moaned loudly, indicating that he was about to spend. Tom gave a final thrust of his hips and let out an exhausted gasp. At that very moment the aching in James's balls became overpoweringly intense, his whole body shuddering, and he could feel the spunk pushing its way upwards. Tank jerked his cock furiously and a jet of semen shot out and landed high up on his chest. This was followed by more shots that gushed from the opening, leaving James powerless to stop himself from being totally emptied. Tom's cock still in his anus intensified the release and spunk splattered over his stomach and dribbled across Tank's hand. It felt as if he would never stop.

Tom pulled his prick from James with a slow movement. He could feel the lad's semen trickling out of him and wetting his throbbing ring. Tank rubbed the remaining come that escaped from James's penis over the sensitive head, making him shiver.

Both Tom and James stayed motionless for a moment in order to regain their breath, still gripped by the potency of the ejaculation. Nobody spoke.

Tom was the first to move, slipping his shining penis back into his underwear and fastening up his breeches. James followed his lead, and slid down from the table, his legs aching from being hoisted so far in the air. His bottom felt sore and wet and he dressed himself with great care. All three boys remained silent, a look of guilt on their faces. James knew that there was something terribly shameful about what had just happened, and yet could not suppress an enormous feeling of naughty enjoyment, as if he were party to the most amazing secret in the world.

When they were dressed the three of them left the barn and

made their way back to the riverbank. Tom and Tank sat down on their shirts and gazed into the tranquil water.

'Are you staying for a swim?' Tank enquired. 'We usually have a dip in the river afterwards. Wash ourselves off and everything.'

James thought for a moment and then shook his head. 'No. I think I'll make my way back now. I don't want to be late for dinner.'

'Fair enough,' said Tank, standing up and beginning to strip off. 'We'll see you later then.'

'Yeah, see you soon,' Tom added, winking a friendly eye.

James gathered his belongings and turned towards the path at the other end of the field. He felt elated by what had just happened, and so lucky to have relations in Rolvenden. What would have happened if he'd never come here was not worth thinking about.

As he neared the bridge that took him away from the river and out into the woods he glanced back, in order to take a final look at his playmates. There they were, beautiful as ever, naked apart from their wet cotton underpants. James smiled to himself and strode back towards Sunningdale.

Everyone was present at dinner that evening. James sat quietly eating his soup, trying not to slurp it. His head was full of thoughts about that afternoon, trying frantically to remember every detail of his initiation into the village lads' gang. A smug look hung across his face. Barnaby glanced at him curiously.

'Why are you looking so pleased with yourself?' he asked.

'No reason,' replied James, with a half smile. 'I'll tell you later.'

'Oh, I see. It's one of *those* kind of things, is it?' Barnaby nodded knowingly and turned back to his food.

Lady Compton-Croft leant across the table in order to speak to James. 'I don't think I've mentioned this to you before – you were probably out drawing or something – but we're

holding a dinner party tomorrow.' She took a sip from her brimming wine glass and awaited a reply.

'That'll be nice,' said James, not quite sure what response he was supposed to give.

'Indeed,' his aunt continued. 'Not a huge gathering, just a few friends. I'm sure it'll be a very pleasant evening.' She paused for a moment. 'And, of course, we'd be delighted if you'd join us.'

'I'd love to.' James adored formal gatherings and found polite chit-chat easy and agreeable. He wondered who would be there and whispered the question into Barnaby's ear, trying not to let his aunt see.

'Oh, a load of old bores, I think,' Barnaby replied in a not altogether quiet enough voice. 'Nobody of any import.' Then a thought struck him. 'Ah, but I do know who'll be waiting on the guests.' He stopped to give James the opportunity to enquire as to who it would be.

'Who?'

'Our friends, Samuel and Gabriel.' He gave James a suggestive look and then whispered, more to himself than anyone else, 'which'll be very pleasant, I'm sure.'

James fell silent. Deep down he was terribly excited at the prospect of both the boys together in the same house as him. However, it was Gabriel that he really wanted to possess, although it seemed an almost impossible thing.

Five

Dressed in his dinner jacket, James made his way down Sunningdale's grand staircase. The drawing room buzzed with the indecipherable chatter of adult voices. James carefully pushed open the door and stepped into the room.

'Ah, James, come in and meet everyone.' Lady Compton-Croft gestured to him with an exuberant flourish of her hand. There were not that many present, but still enough to appear daunting to James. He shook the hand of each person as he was introduced to them and exchanged a polite how-do-you-do, before moving on to the next. The only person outside the family that he recognised was Gerald Albemarle who loitered in a corner submerged in conversation with Barnaby. He could not see Samuel Grainger or Gabriel Wood anywhere, even though his cousin had told him that they would be acting as waiters tonight. James had dressed in his finest clothes so as to look his best for them.

He crossed to where his cousin and the professor were standing and greeted them.

'James, my dear, how are you? We were just talking about

you.' Barnaby smiled in his usual charming manner and put a friendly arm around James's shoulder.

'What were you saying?' James asked, a little taken aback at the thought of being spoken about.

'Oh, nothing in particular.' James looked a little curious, forcing Barnaby to elaborate. 'I was just telling Gerald about your love of art, and how wonderful I thought your paintings to be.' James blushed with modesty. 'The professor was expressing a great interest in taking a look at them at some point.' Barnaby glanced across at the man in question. 'Weren't you, Gerald?'

'Yes, indeed. They sound *most* interesting.' He stared at James with an enthusiastic smile. 'Especially your most recent . . .' he paused, searching for the correct word, 'portraits.'

James looked at Barnaby, his eyes wide as if asking a silent question, not quite sure whether the professor was referring to what he thought he was referring to. Barnaby said nothing.

'I can't imagine what you mean, Professor Albemarle,' James said in an innocent tone.

'Come, come now, James, I'm sure you do.' This was enough to throw a cold silence over the conversation. James felt rather uneasy at the thought of his shameful exploits being discussed with the professor. It felt as if his cousin were continually indulging in private jokes at his expense. However, there was something about the relaxed ways of the village that made James feel a little more comfortable with people finding out about his secret passions. He was grateful that the strictness of London and its proper society behaviour seemed to have little relevance in Rolvenden.

'You haven't got a drink, James,' Professor Albemarle noticed, glancing down at James's empty hands. 'Where are those servants?' He glanced around the room with a searching look.

'Yes, I wonder what's taking them so long,' said Barnaby. James's attention was immediately pulled back from his own

private thoughts. 'I think Samuel went to get the hors-d'oeuvres, and Gabriel's down in the cellar fetching another bottle of Scotch.'

James could not suppress the grin that crept out and across his face. It thrilled James inside to know that he would be able to watch them all evening, serving drinks and food, waiting on the guests and looking restrained, but beautiful, in their black and white uniforms.

'Ah, here's Gabriel now.' The doors opened and in stepped the boy himself, looking, James thought, more lovely than ever. It seemed that every time he set eyes on Gabriel it was like the first time, his body convulsed with the sensation, like acciden-tally touching something that was burning hot, and jumping back in pain. However, the emotions that lit his senses were not painful. They were like a lovely revelation, at once devastatingly elating, and yet also revealing of a frightening truth.

He was dressed, as James expected, in the usual garb of a servant waiting at a formal dinner or party. A white shirt, highly starched, black trousers and bow tie, and a gold-coloured waistcoat, buttoned up all the way. These clothes though, however formal, could not conceal the lad's beautiful body, his smooth torso – the memory of which filled James's mind – his strong upper arms and tight, rounded buttocks. James pictured him serving the drinks naked, and wished that the roomful of people would disappear and they could be left alone to explore one another's bodies.

Barnaby beckoned him over with a shout. 'Can we have some more drinks over here?' Gabriel came straight across. 'Ah, there you are. We were all wondering where you'd got to.'

'I'd just gone to fetch some more bottles, sir,' Gabriel replied in a humble tone.

'Of course you did. That's right.' Barnaby helped himself to a gin-martini cocktail from the tray and laid a reassuring arm across Gabriel's back as he did so. 'You remember James, don't you?'

102

'Yes, indeed, sir,' said Gabriel, and he smiled tenderly at him. This thrilled James no end.

'How are you?' he asked, coming close up to the boy and taking a drink.

'I'm fine, sir,' replied Gabriel. Barnaby threw a look at James, as if to say 'I'll leave you two alone,' and he turned his back on the boys and began a conversation with Professor Albemarle.

'I really enjoyed our walk around the village the other day,' James began. 'We'll have to do it again sometime.'

'Yes, I'd like that.' There was something in the enthusiasm of his response that excited James. He sounded really eager, which made him think that perhaps the lad might be open to persuasion.

'I was also wondering whether . . .' James tried to be as casual as he could, 'at some point, you'd like to pose for me again.' He added, 'If you want to, that is,' to try to make out that he wasn't that bothered.

'Of course I'll pose for you.' James breathed a sigh of relief. 'Every artist needs a model.'

'Thank you.' The boys smiled at one another and James felt as if he had really found a friend in Gabriel. 'I'm not quite sure how to put this, but . . .' James took in a deep breath and chose his words carefully, 'when artists draw their models they often draw them . . . without their clothes on.'

'I suppose you're right.'

'Just so they can get a good idea of what the male physique really looks like.' James attempted to put his words into some sort of sensible artistic context. He did not want the boy to think he was making an improper suggestion, even if he was.

'Oh, I see.' Gabriel had finally caught on to what James was proposing. A look of thoughtful consideration came over his face.

'Think about it,' James said. 'You don't have to if you don't want to.'

'All right. I'll think about it. But I've got to get back to

serving these drinks now, sir, so if you'll excuse me.' James watched the lad's beautifully shaped bottom move off into the crowd of guests, and wondered whether he had offended or frightened him. He would seek him out tomorrow and see what his decision was about posing nude, but he hoped and prayed that the answer would be yes.

Barnaby came back over to where James was standing and handed him another cocktail. 'Here, try this.'

'What is it?' James asked.

'Gin and Dubonnet. Simply all the rage at the moment. Well, with me at least,' he added, clinking his own glass against James's. 'Cheers! So how was Gabriel? You *do* seem terribly fond of him.'

James knew that he could hide nothing from his cousin, and felt at ease sharing his desires with him. They were alike in many ways and both appreciated the company of boys. 'Yes, he's lovely. But he's got a girl, so I don't know how I'll ever have him.'

'So what? You know what boys are like. And anyway, everyone's persuadable. You just have to be patient . . . and crafty,' he added.

'I hope you're right. I suppose it was the case with the boys down by the river.' James sighed at the mere thought of those lovely lads, letting their boyish urges run free and be satiated.

'Tom and Tank you mean?' Barnaby asked with a cheeky smile on his face. 'Yes, they're very broad-minded.'

'Do you know them too?'

'Oh, indeed I do.' Barnaby laughed so loudly that one or two of the guests standing close by looked around to see what was so funny. 'So you've been there too? Good for you.'

'Yes,' James replied with a slightly boastful tone, pleased to have something to be proud of. 'And it was very nice too.'

'I'm sure it was. Perhaps we ought to invite them over tomorrow evening.' Barnaby looked at James cautiously. 'What do you think?'

'Yes, why not. As long as *you* make the arrangements.' James tried to look calm and collected, as if the lads were just trivial distractions, but deep down he was bubbling with excitement at the possibility of having them again. Perhaps this time they might allow him to linger over their bodies, explore them a little more, and give a little more back.

As he thought about the two boys, Sam entered the room bearing a tray of hors-d'oeuvres, and they caught one another's eye. A faint smile of acknowledgement flickered across the boy's face. He was dressed in the same fashion as Gabriel, and looked cute and boyish, the uniform giving him an air of social detachment and unavailability. James and Barnaby exchanged a conspiratorial smile.

After dinner the guests processed from the dining room and into the drawing room. The meal had been pleasant and James felt a little drunk, what with the cocktails and then the wine. He was not used to drinking so much alcohol. At home such pleasures were reserved for his father and special occasions. James was also curious as to what his cousin was planning. He was sure that he had seen him subtly slip a piece of paper into Sam's waistcoat pocket while he was pouring the dessert wine. However, this could have been nothing more than a flick of Barnaby's napkin or the effect of the drink.

Barnaby poured himself and James two large whiskies and they sat down in armchairs at the far side of the room.

'Now, we've got to be able to slip away without anyone noticing us,' he said, glancing at his watch. 'Especially my mother.'

'What are you talking about?' James looked confused. 'Slip away where?' Even though he was far from sober, there was something in his cousin's scheming tone of voice that reminded him of the summer-house expedition. Perhaps he had something similar planned.

Barnaby ignored him. 'There's just enough time to finish

these and then we need to make our escape.' James decided that it was best to go along with him and see where it all led. It surely would be more fun than being trapped in a dull conversation with his aunt or Professor Albemarle. 'And remind me to grab a bottle of whisky on the way out.' Barnaby paused, as an idea struck him. 'In fact . . . Gabriel!' he called as the boy passed by.

'Yes, sir.'

'Would you do me a favour and bring a bottle of Scotch over?'

'Very good, sir.' And within a few seconds Barnaby was secreting the bottle under his dinner jacket and making a movement towards the door.

'Come on then. It's almost ten o'clock,' he hissed over his shoulder at James.

'Where are you off to, darling?' the shrill voice of Lady Compton-Croft enquired, never one to miss a trick.

'James and I are just taking a stroll around the garden, Mother,' Barnaby replied in a guileless voice. 'We won't be long.'

'Oh, Barny, you are terrible.' But the boys had already left the room.

James followed his cousin up the stairs and towards the area of the house where their bedrooms were located. Barnaby placed a hand on the door knob and froze for a second in order to throw a look back at James before entering the room.

Sam sat on the bed, still dressed in his servant's clothes. As they entered he stood up. 'You didn't tell me you'd be bringing anyone else.'

'It's only James. I'm sure it's nothing he hasn't seen before.' Barnaby approached the boy and ran his hand through the lad's thick floppy hair. James stood silently watching, wondering what would happen next. His prick began to harden at the thought of what intrigues may be in store for the boy.

'Right. I think we ought to play a little game. One of my

106

favourites,' Barnaby said, stepping a few paces back from where Sam was standing. 'What do you think, James?'

'Whatever you want,' James replied in a nervous voice.

'I'll take that as a "yes" then.' He locked the door, took his jacket off and rolled up the sleeves of his shirt. 'Let's play doctor and patient. James, you can be my assistant.' He sat in a chair next to the bed. James felt excited at the idea, but was unsure as to what exactly the game entailed. 'Right,' Barnaby took on a tone of authority, as if he really was a doctor. 'I think we're going to have to take a look at you. A thorough examination is what you need.'

'Yes, sir.' As if they had played the game many times before, Sam entered into the situation, and in doing so, looked like a little boy standing expectantly in the surgery awaiting examination.

'I'm afraid you're going to have to strip. I need to take a close look at you.' Barnaby remained seated. 'Remove your waistcoat and shirt, please.' Sam did so and was beckoned towards the doctor. His smooth chest and stomach looked as lovely to James as it had that night in the summer house. Barnaby ran his hands all over it, exploring every muscle and piece of flesh, making Sam raise his arms in order to examine the fine hairs underneath and turning him around and feeling his muscular back and shoulders. James's cock stood stiff as iron and he could feel a trickle of sticky fluid wetting his underwear.

'That's fine. Now take off your breeches, shoes and socks.' Sam once again silently complied, slowly removing the formal restrictions of his uniform. From where James stood he had a splendid view of the lad's pert buttocks, the material at the centre of his underwear trapped between the cheeks, and it was easy to imagine what his arse would look like when exposed.

Barnaby took hold of the boy by the hips and angled him closely towards his seated position. He was at liberty to thoroughly examine him now. 'Right. I'm just going to take a look at your balls. Check that everything's in order.' He

107

carefully slipped Sam's white cotton undershorts down, only at the front, and let them sit just below his tight sack. The boy's cock looked thick and powerful, even though it was flaccid. His glands were large and tensed. Barnaby let a cold-looking medical hand investigate Sam's balls. He squeezed them with his palm, rolling them around in order to explore every aspect. 'Cough,' he instructed, and Sam coughed.

James had never understood why doctors always asked boys to cough while they were feeling their balls, and the show before him brought him no closer to an explanation. His own cock though throbbed painfully and he longed to touch Sam in the way his cousin did.

'Now let's take a little look at your penis.' Barnaby let go of the lad's balls and took a hold of his cock. The member quivered in his hands, Sam clearly no longer able to contain his sexual excitement. With care, and yet at the same time with a thorough investigative coldness, Barnaby retracted the lad's foreskin and exposed the shiny head beneath. He then put a thumb either side of the tip and stretched the skin back, making the entrance dilate and a small amount of clear fluid seep out. Sam sucked in a breath, as if he was in a slight amount of pain, and gripped the tops of his legs to steady himself.

'That seems fine,' Barnaby said, letting the boy's cock go. 'Now I need to take a look at your bottom,' looking Sam in the eye as he spoke. 'I'll give you a quick check-up here,' he indicated the place where he sat, 'and then I may need to do a deeper examination afterwards.' Sam nodded as if to say he understood.

With an expert touch Barnaby turned his patient around and slowly pulled the back of his underpants down until they rested just below his taut buttocks. James stared at the display before him, transfixed. Sam looked so innocent and his cousin so masterful. He longed for the time when it would be his turn to play a part in the scene.

With both hands placed on the lad's firm cheeks, Barnaby

gently rubbed and squeezed them from where he sat, his face a couple of inches from the objects in question. 'Now, if you can just bend over and touch your toes . . .' Sam complied, bending the top half of his body downwards as far as it would go. Barnaby was left with unrestricted access to the boy's most intimate crevice.

From a drawer in the table beside the bed he produced a tub of Vaseline, which he unscrewed and dipped a finger in. The digit looked cold and slimy in the dim light of his bedroom, and menacing in the way that everyday things that aren't supposed to, often are.

'This may feel a little uncomfortable, but it won't be too painful.' He parted the buttocks and James caught a glimpse of Sam's tight, pink arsehole. Barnaby held the boy steady and open with one hand and allowed the tip of his lubricated finger to pierce the lad's anal opening. Sam groaned a little as the digit slid right inside him, up to the knuckle. James watched as his cousin twisted the finger around and probed deeply into the lad's interior. He imagined how the tight anal muscles must feel as they clamped around the intruding probe.

As suddenly as he had pushed it in, he pulled it out again. Sam sighed a little as the digital examination ended and stood upright once more. Barnaby slapped him playfully on the bottom and told him that he could pull his underpants back up. Sam did so, and his penis looked hard as a rock back inside his underwear.

'Right, Sam, I'm afraid we're going to have to make a more thorough examination.' Barnaby stood up. 'If you'd like to hop onto the bed and lie down on your back, then we can get started.' Sam obeyed and laid himself flat out over the bed, his hands, palms facing down, at his sides. 'James, perhaps you could assist me at this point.' James had been wondering when the opportunity would arise for him to take part in the examination. Now was his chance.

'Let's take these off,' said Barnaby, sliding Sam's underpants

down and putting them on the chair. The lad lay back and left himself open to what was about to happen. 'Now, I need you to raise you legs in the air.' Sam lifted his legs. 'Spread them.' Sam did so. Barnaby took up the jar of Vaseline once more and lubricated his fingers. James watched as his cousin parted the cheeks as widely as he could and rubbed a hand over Sam's exposed entrance. Then he massaged a small amount of the greasy substance over the puckered lips of the lad's arsehole and gradually began to ease a finger into his anus.

Sam's stomach muscles tensed and he took in a large gulp of breath. Barnaby pushed the finger all the way in, and then added a second, stretching open the boy's tight hole and allowing his fingers to move freely in and out. Sam began to moan and his penis stiffened once again into a large erection. Due to the enlarging of the head of the cock, the foreskin glided back and exposed the slippery, purple knob.

'James, could you give me a hand and examine Sam's penis, while I continue at this end?' James nodded enthusiastically and took hold of the straining erection. He knew exactly what to do and lifted the cock up and began to stimulate the shaft by moving the foreskin backwards and forwards across the head. At the same time Barnaby slid two more fingers into Sam's dilated hole and worked them right up inside. He frigged them back and forth, the force of which encouraged a trickle of sticky liquid to ooze from the tip of Sam's prick. James masturbated the lad as roughly as he could and Sam panted beneath their molesting hands. He let his other hand wander across the lad's chest, investigating his smooth torso and gently squeezing his hard nipples.

At that moment the pleasure of having his cock wanked and his prostate stimulated became too much for Sam and his balls tightened and his cock became as hard as it ever would. James knew that Sam was about to come and wanked him furiously. Overtaken with desire James moved forward and let his lips engulf the end of the lad's prick just in time to be able to catch

a long spurt of spunk as it shot from the tip. He gulped it down greedily. The semen continued to flow from Sam's cock and James lapped it all up. He could taste its saltiness as it hit the back of his throat. He loved the idea of draining the lad of all his fluid, leaving him exhausted and spent. As the thick member emptied itself into his mouth, he could feel it straining upwards, urged on by the pressure of Barnaby's fingers thrust up inside Sam's arse.

As the final drops of sperm oozed out James could feel Sam panting heavily beneath him. He was exhausted. Barnaby slid his finger out of the lad's arsehole and James stopped sucking, his mouth now full of the gorgeous taste of the boy's spunk. Sam took his underwear from the chair and slipped them back on, still breathless from the thorough examination.

'Well,' Barnaby sighed, 'everything seems to be in working order. Scotch anyone?'

James ran down the stairs and back into the drawing room. He did not want anyone to get suspicious and by now his aunt would certainly be aware of his absence. It was almost midnight and most of the guests had gone home.

'James, where on earth have you been?' said Lady Compton-Croft.

'Oh, I'm sorry, we must have got carried away,' James said, his face the picture of innocence. 'We were engrossed in some conversation about art or something. And it's such a fine night. You ought to take a stroll yourself.'

'No, thank you.' His aunt gave him a disapproving glance. 'And where's Barnaby?'

'Oh, he's still outside.'

'Outside? At midnight?' Lady Compton-Croft did not believe him for a moment. 'That boy will be the death of me.'

The party thinned out even more and James soon found himself virtually alone in the room. He sat in the window seat, with a drink and the soft warm summer night breeze drifting in

through the open window. He felt drunk and happy. Thoughts of his exploits earlier with his cousin and Sam gave him an excited glow inside. The servants had all been dismissed and the house was silent. At the opposite end of the room his aunt and Gerald Albemarle sat talking in hushed voices and James was thinking about Gabriel. How lovely he had looked tonight in his smart clothes and polished shoes, and how lovely he must look out of them. James imagined how wonderful it would be to caress his naked body, kiss his secret parts and taste his seed, as he had done with Sam not half an hour earlier.

He wondered whether, due to the late hour of the party's end, the hired village servants might have been allowed to sleep over. James plucked up the courage to ask his aunt.

'Aunt Cordelia, are the servants from the village staying in the house tonight?'

'Yes, I think so,' she looked confused. 'Why do you ask?'

'No reason, I was just concerned that it was a long way for them to walk back at this time of night.'

'Samuel and Gabriel are both sleeping in the servants' quarters. Gabriel usually goes home after his odd-job-boy duties are done in the morning, but tonight he's staying here.' Lady Compton-Croft shook her head as if in despair at such silly questions.

James had an idea. He would pay Gabriel a visit. The alcohol he had consumed bolstered his confidence and he wished his aunt a pleasant night's sleep and made his way along the corridor and down the stairs to the lower level of the house where some of the servants slept. He had a good idea where he might be able to find the boy and he hoped he would still be awake. As James approached the room where he thought Gabriel might be staying he noticed that the door was open an inch, so he peered inside. As he suspected he saw the figure of his friend lying on the bed. James carefully pushed open the door and slipped into the room.

'Are you awake?' James whispered, not wanting to disturb

him if he wasn't. 'Gabriel?' There was no reply. He moved closer to the side of the bed and looked down through the gloom at the lad's sleeping face. He must be exhausted, thought James, after having to serve all evening. He could not help but linger a little over the boy's beautiful features captured in the moonlight that fell through a crack in the curtains. Gabriel was lying stretched out on his back and breathing softly. James knelt down beside the bed in order to look more closely. It was then that he noticed the lad was not wearing anything on top, probably because it was such a warm night. Beside the bed, on the back of a chair, lay Gabriel's clothes: his smart trousers and waistcoat, his shirt, and lying on the floor, a pair of cotton underpants.

James felt extremely excited at the sight of his love asleep – defenceless and unaware of his presence – with his underwear right there in front of him. He was still on edge after sucking Sam's cock and the sight of the sleeping boy was enough to make his own prick grow stiff. He wondered whether Gabriel was naked beneath the sheets and stared hard at the area where the lad's genitals would be. There was a bulge in the covers and James leaned forward a fraction to take a look. In the dim light he could just make out the shape of the lad's cock and balls below his flat stomach.

Suddenly Gabriel let out a tired groan and James moved back in case he woke up. He watched as the lad shifted his position in the bed, turning his back on James, and once again settling down into silent sleep. Sexually excited and liberated from inhibition by the alcohol he summoned up his courage and sat down in the chair beside the bed. He gazed down at the pair of underpants lying on the floor and wondered what they might smell like.

James remembered his shameful expeditions into the changing rooms when he was a schoolboy. He'd wait until the other boys had changed for games, then he'd sneak in and sniff their underwear, making a special effort to find the ones of the boys

113

he liked most. It was naughty and wrong, but the aroma of their crotches filled James's nostrils and he was transported to a private world of ecstasy. Occasionally he would steal a pair and keep them hidden in his study room, bringing them out every now and again to sniff at while masturbating.

All these memories passed through his head now as he stared down at Gabriel's underwear lying before him. He could not resist just taking a little look at them. Checking that the boy was indeed asleep he carefully bent down and picked them up. They were made of fine, white cotton, had an elasticated waistband and buttons down the front, providing access to his genitals. They were creased and slightly tatty, obviously from having been worn many times. Just holding them gave James the feeling that he had somehow been allowed, by default, a special amount of admittance to an otherwise private zone.

James examined the material more closely. He could make out a faint bulge at the front where the cotton had been stretched over Gabriel's cock and balls, and at the back a crease where it must have slipped between his buttocks. He took a deep breath and placed the frontal area to his nose, inhaling deeply, his eyes closed. They were still very slightly warm from the lad's body, having obviously only been recently removed, and the aroma was heavenly. A delicious musky odour filled James's nostrils, pungent and exciting, and he sniffed again. No trace of Gabriel's real smell had been lost in their removal. They smelt sweaty and slightly dirty, the lad's heavy balls having been confined in the folds of material all day. Most excitingly of all, where the tip of his cock would have rested there were the traces of a sticky liquid. Perhaps the boy's pent-up sexual anxiety from the day's work had resulted in a dribble of pre-come spilling out from the end of his knob. James could not restrain himself and he tasted the fluid with the tip of his tongue. It was sticky and salty, and made his own cock twitch violently in his trousers. It was agony not to caress himself as he sniffed at Gabriel's underpants, and he slipped his penis out and

114

gently tugged at the foreskin. The aroma of the underwear was so stimulating that he knew it would not take long before he ejaculated.

James pictured Gabriel's heavy sack clamped tightly into the material and inhaled deeply. What a joy it would be to actually lick the balls themselves and not just their imprint. From the smell James could guess what the lad's genitals would actually taste of. At this very moment they were lying in the bed, warm and musky, while James only had the memory of them to sniff at.

He moved the underpants away from his nose and looked once again at the back where Gabriel's bottom had been positioned throughout the day. This part seemed even more taboo than the crotch area, and to sniff here was the ultimate intimacy. He felt nervous even thinking about it, and checked to see whether the lad was still asleep. He was, so James lifted the back of the underwear up to his face and stretched out the creased material that had slipped in between Gabriel's buttocks in order to fully inhale the odour. His cock felt as if it would explode as the aroma of the boy's most sensitive and unavailable spot filled his nostrils. He tugged at his prick as hard as he could.

There was a muskiness here too, but different to that of the frontal area, and a strong smell of sweat. James could picture Gabriel's arse cheeks rubbing together all day in the hot material, becoming warm and tense, their scent still strongly embedded in the thin cotton. He sniffed deeply and imagined that he was inhaling Gabriel's crack. It was a profound notion that this material had spent all day trapped in the lad's hairy groove. A lovely place, James thought, to spend one's day.

James could feel his cock pulsating in his hand; he would come at any moment. He let the underwear fall to the floor and stopped wanking himself. He did not want his seed to spill out, just in case Gabriel awoke and caught him in such a compromising position. Out of breath, James toyed with the

idea of leaving the room and going to bed, but he was too fired up to desert the sleeping boy. He gazed down at him and as he did so the lad shifted his position once more, so that now he was lying face down, his arms and legs spread out on the mattress, sound asleep. The sheet that had covered Gabriel's back had slipped down and rested just above his buttocks, which jutted out, firm and round.

The mixture of alcohol and sexual desire was too much for James and he felt wild and out of control. He could not restrain himself – Gabriel lying there so enticingly – and he allowed his hand to brush the sleeping boy's back and waist. For a brief moment he felt sure that the lad would wake up and be angry with him, but Gabriel did not even stir. Bolstered by the lack of reaction to his caresses, James summoned up the courage to continue. His confidence and desire encouraged one another to explore further. Surely there could be no harm in taking advantage of the lad while he slept? What he did not know would not bother him. And perhaps, James thought, this would be the only way he would ever get to touch him. Although he felt brave his hands still shook with fear as they gently stroked the small of Gabriel's back. He did not want to be discovered.

James sucked in a deep breath and rubbed the hollow between Gabriel's back and the top of his buttocks. The sheet was only inches away from revealing what he had for so long wanted to see, and he allowed his hand to stray underneath. He could feel the delicate line of hair in the cleft of the lad's arse cheeks – that lovely point where the two globes came together. James knew that this line led down the crack and eventually to Gabriel's arsehole.

With the greatest care, not wanting to wake the peaceful lad, James pulled the sheet back and revealed his naked buttocks. It was such a warm night that Gabriel would not notice the lack of covers. The light from the moon lit his cheeks as they projected out, sharply distinct from his smooth, muscular back and the hairy tops of his legs. They looked firm and round and

James ran his hands over their smooth surface. Even though Gabriel was asleep and relaxed, his buttocks remained tensed. James felt overcome with desire and could not resist putting his face close to them and inhaling their faint musk.

Checking that Gabriel was still sleeping, James took advantage of his situation and gently kissed the lad's bottom. The sensation was so divine that he continued to kiss the soft flesh all over, exploring and mapping out all aspects of the lad's arse, trying to remember every detail for later recollection. As he roamed over the cheeks James noticed the tiniest droplets of perspiration where they met at the top and he could not resist licking these off. The sweat tasted of his beloved Gabriel and it was amazing.

He had come this far, so going further seemed easy. With the softest motion James let his tongue run the length of Gabriel's crack. As he licked at the fine hairs either side his nose parted the buttocks and, for the first time, was able to take in the lad's real smell. It was even more pungent than the trace left on his underwear. A sweet and musky stench mixed with a trace of sweat invaded James's nostrils and made him feel quite faint. This was the aroma of his beloved's most private parts.

James placed a thumb either side of Gabriel's arse cheeks and delicately prised them apart. The faint smell grew stronger and he lowered his face closer to the soft crack that now opened before him. Ever so gently James sniffed the hole itself. It looked tight and muscled, with a soft ring of hair surrounding it, the opening almost imperceptible. Holding the buttocks apart with one hand, James wetted the forefinger of his other hand with a small amount of saliva and ran the tip over Gabriel's arsehole. The puckered hole opened slightly like a sleepy eye and swallowed the end of James's finger. It felt warm and slippery inside the anal passage, and Gabriel's muscles tightened, as if they did not want to let go.

James removed the finger and immediately replaced it with his tongue. The smell and taste of Gabriel's arse mingled in his

mouth and he gently lapped away at the muscled crack between the lad's buttocks. His tongue moved up and down the crease, but soon came to rest back on the tender hole. With every careful dab of his tongue the once-tight ring became more relaxed, and was soon dilated enough for James to slide effortlessly inside. The smell became increasingly potent with every lick.

Without warning a groan of sleepy pleasure slipped from Gabriel's mouth. James paused in order to make sure that the lad had not awoken before continuing to probe more deeply, the inside of the buttocks now wet with his saliva and his face jammed between them.

James pulled the sheet down even further and stroked the top of the lad's legs. They were thick and covered with dark hair, and parted enough to allow access to his perineum area. James was also able to see the back of his scrotum. The balls looked hefty and threatening and were shrouded in dark, wiry hair. He moved his tongue down the thick strip of muscle and onto Gabriel's balls. There was a sweaty taste at the base of them and James lapped gently in order to absorb every drop.

His attentions, however, soon returned to Gabriel's arsehole, and he re-inserted his tongue in the slippery opening. As he licked in and out of the passage and all around the ring he used his hands to hold apart and caress the buttocks. James thought how lovely the lad looked spread out and asleep, while his tongue violated the unconscious boy, dipping into him, taking advantage of the situation.

All of a sudden there came another moan from Gabriel's lips, and James pulled away just in time for the lad to turn over onto his back. James remained motionless, holding his breath in for almost a minute. If Gabriel had woken up with all the tickling movements of James's tongue, then he wanted to make out as if he was not there. There was complete silence and James took a peek at the lad's face. It looked as it had done before: peaceful and asleep, a gentle smile curving the sides of his mouth.

118

James re-assessed the situation and was instantly shocked by what he saw. Gabriel was lying on his back, almost completely uncovered, with the biggest erection jutting up from him. James closed his eyes for a moment to make sure that he was not dreaming, but when he opened them once again the lad's stiff cock was still there. Although asleep, it was as if Gabriel was inviting attention, beckoning James towards the centre-piece of his gorgeous form. He did not know why the lad should be so hard when asleep. Perhaps it was just that most teenagers got excited in the night and Gabriel was no exception, or maybe, James wondered, it was because of his soft kisses. Perhaps in his sleepy state he was revealing his true desires, or maybe just the cravings of an aroused boy.

The sight was all too much for James, and there was no question of self-control or restraint in a case like this. He could do nothing but obey his most natural instincts and take the lad in his mouth. How he had dreamt about this moment, dwelt on the act of gently pleasuring Gabriel.

With a careful hand James caressed the youth's stomach. The muscles were tight and conspicuous, and a feathery covering of hair surrounded his navel. His hands slid down Gabriel's abdomen and towards the ultimate goal – the lad's thick penis. The thing quivered there above a cloud of dark pubic hair, its foreskin still covering the head. James was amazed at how such a young man could have such a huge penis.

James moved himself into a comfortable kneeling position at the side of the bed, and leant across so that his mouth was in line with the top of Gabriel's prick. With his left hand he cautiously took a hold of the organ and gradually pulled the foreskin back, not wanting to awaken the lad with too swift a motion. The end glistened, sticky and hard, and James stretched the skin back as far as it would go until it was possible to see the thin strands that held the foreskin in place. The purple-coloured helmet seemed to pulsate in the moonlight now that it had been exposed. James prepared himself for the ultimate

transgression, and parting his lips, allowed them to glide over the tip of Gabriel's cock. He clasped the base of the member and let it slide inside as far as it could. It was almost impossible to get it all in; so bulky was it that James had to stretch his mouth as widely as he could.

He sucked gently at first, not wanting the tickling sensation of his tongue passing over the head to wake the lad. With every downward movement James's nostrils were filled with Gabriel's most lovely aroma, the same aroma as he had inhaled in the underpants left discarded on the floor, except more pungent – the same difference as there is between a lady's perfume and a vase of roses. The lad's boyish smell was a combination of cheap soap, musky body odour and acrid, manly sweat. James breathed the fragrance in as he let his mouth massage the head of the prick. Very softly he cupped Gabriel's balls in his left hand and allowed his head to make all the stimulating movements.

James was not sure what all this would lead to. Surely the lad would not be able to spend in his sleep? However, as he sucked a trace of a sticky emission oozed out of the tip and onto James's tongue – a precursor for the final release. It tasted so lovely that James dissolved into the act of stimulating Gabriel's smooth head so completely that he no longer cared whether bringing the lad to his crisis would wake him or not. With ever-increasingly swift movements James forced the lad towards a climax. There was a difference in his breathing patterns: once James had heard long, deep inhalations of air, now they were short and panted, as if he were having a disturbing dream. Gabriel seemed so relaxed in sleep that it was possible to make him come without too much effort, and James felt him shake a little, an exhausted moan coming from his lips. Then the head of his prick became rock hard and he shuddered.

James felt a long, lovely spurt of salty discharge shoot out of the tip of Gabriel's prick and into his mouth. He gulped it down, the taste sending a shiver up his spine. More short spasms followed and James's mouth filled with semen, more than he

could swallow in one go. He could feel the lad's balls trembling with the rhythmic ejaculating of his viscous juices.

When Gabriel's cock had finished spurting James let it carefully slide out of his mouth and relinquished his grasp on the lad's heavy glands. He looked up just in time to see him opening one eye and stretching a lazy arm. James immediately moved back from the bed and threw the sheet over Gabriel's still-erect cock. Gabriel sat up in bed with a start.

'What are you doing here, sir?' he said, still half-asleep.

'I . . . I was . . .' James stuttered, searching for an excuse. 'I just came in to see how you were.' He was terrified that he had been found out. Would Gabriel suddenly realise what had been going on and alert his aunt? 'Sorry, I didn't realise you were asleep. I'll leave you alone.' James got up and crossed to the door.

'I must have been having a bit of a dream.' Gabriel yawned and closed his eyes once more. 'A very nice dream it was too.'

James opened the door. 'Goodnight,' he whispered and slipped out of the room. He could still taste Gabriel's semen at the back of his throat as he climbed the stairs and went into his bedroom, and for a moment he savoured it, thinking that perhaps it might be the first and only time he would ever be able to consume his love's sweet seed.

Six

———

'Where did you disappear off to last night?' said Barnaby between mouthfuls of toast. 'I came to speak to you and you weren't in your room.'

'Oh, nowhere. I just went out for a bit of a stroll, that's all.' James was damned if he was going to reveal his guilty secret, even to his cousin. There was something too shameful about taking advantage of a sleeping boy, and he did not want Barnaby to think him corrupt.

'I see.'

James sipped at his tea and looked out of the breakfast-room window. It was a bright, cheerful Wednesday and he hoped to be able to find Gabriel after breakfast and see whether he would honour his promise of posing for him. 'What are you doing today?' James asked his cousin.

'Not terribly much. I have some research to do,' Barnaby said glancing up from his newspaper. 'As you know it's my final year at Oxford, and I've lots of work. But it all seems so trivial on a beautiful day like this. I may take a walk down to the river and see if the boys are around.' He looked a little smug as his eyes lowered towards the morning's headlines.

'Tom and Tank you mean?' James asked in a hoarse whisper.

'Yes. So make sure you're around this evening. They might be persuaded to come and visit us.'

Lady Compton-Croft glared across the table. 'Who's that you're talking about, darling?'

'No one, Mother.' Barnaby shot her a disgruntled look, which was enough to silence her. 'Nothing to do with you.'

'When do you think they'll be coming?' James enquired.

'I don't know. I'll tell you at dinner.'

After breakfast James asked one of the maids where he could find Gabriel. She pointed to the scullery and he made his way along the dark kitchen corridor. He pushed the scullery door open and there was Gabriel, stacking crates in a corner of the damp room.

'Hello,' said James.

Gabriel spun around. 'You made me jump.'

'I'm sorry, I didn't mean to. I was just wondering whether you were free to pose for me today?' James let his face look a little pleading. 'You said you would.'

'Oh, sir, I completely forgot all about that. I've got to work this morning and afternoon, then I've promised to spend the rest of the day with my girl,' Gabriel replied.

James's heart instantly sank, the disappointment showing itself on his face. He could not allow himself to be pushed aside for things that seemed so unimportant to him – work and women.

'If I asked my aunt whether you could have an hour or so off, then I could draw you and after that you could go and see your girl.' James found it almost impossible to pronounce the last two words without sneering a little.

'Well, if her ladyship don't mind . . .' Gabriel hardly had time to finish his sentence.

'That's settled then. I'll go and ask her.' James ran out of the door and in the direction of his aunt's rooms.

★　★　★

At three o'clock James was waiting by the entrance to the servants' quarters for Gabriel to come out. Lady Compton-Croft had said that it was all right for him to leave his duties an hour early. She was eager to encourage James's art and glad to be able to provide him with a model. What she did not know, however, was that James had more shameful motives for requesting Gabriel's time than just artistic ones.

The door was pushed open and Gabriel stood erect and ready in his shabby clothes and heavy boots, a naive expression on his face. 'Are you sure this is all fine with your aunt?'

'Yes. Now let's get going if we've only got an hour.' James led the way upstairs to his bedroom.

'Where are we going?' Gabriel asked.

'To my room. It's the only place where we'll get any privacy.' James looked back and smiled at his friend. 'Are you sure you still want to do this?'

There was a nervous look about the lad and James worried that perhaps he would not want to take all his clothes off and pose. 'Yes. I said I would and I'm a man of my word.'

James tingled all over at the word 'man' coming from Gabriel's lips. It was so sweet to hear someone so young claiming to be a man. James never felt like a man, just a child trapped in a world where he must from now on pretend to be anything but a child.

James pushed open the door to his bedroom and gestured for Gabriel to enter. 'Well, we may as well get started straight away.' He gathered together his paper and pencils and seated himself in an armchair by the window. 'Why don't you stand there,' James said waving a hand towards the other side of the room and a small chest of drawers. Gabriel moved across and stood where James had indicated. He took his jacket off and dropped it onto the floor. He was standing now in a black waistcoat, white shirt and grey canvas breeches. Looking directly at James he carefully removed the waistcoat and laid it down on top of his jacket.

James remained motionless, watching every movement his friend was making, wondering whether the lad would strip without hesitation, or whether he would need to coax him out of his clothes.

'Shall I take my shirt off now?' Gabriel asked with an innocent voice.

'Yes,' James replied, and his penis began stiffening. He watched as the lad unbuttoned the front of his top and let it slide from his shoulders and onto the floor. His body was as inviting as it had been the previous night as he lay asleep in bed and James had taken advantage of his most intimate areas. Gabriel's chest was smooth and hard, his nipples stuck out like stiff little buttons and the tight stomach muscles ran in lines beneath the skin.

Gabriel eyed James, as if to say 'is this all right?' and James smiled a warm and pleasing smile. The lad seemed to be slightly more at ease and James hoped that he would feel more able to remove his clothes.

Gabriel stood motionless for a moment, posed in the afternoon light that flooded in through James's bedroom window. There was also a soft breeze from the open casement which gently ruffled the lad's fringe. His hair was closely cropped at the sides, drawing attention to his ears, which stuck out slightly. James thought this made him look even more adorable, and he stared hard into his deep chestnut-brown eyes. 'Do you want me to take these off now?' he said, pointing to his breeches. James nodded. Gabriel stooped over and removed his heavy boots and thick socks. These were followed by his trousers, which he let fall to the floor. After standing still for a moment he stepped out of them and pushed them aside with his bare foot.

James stared in rapture at the lad before him and his prick stood up stiffly in his trousers. He adjusted his shirt and sat back a little in the chair so as to keep his erection hidden from Gabriel; he wanted nothing to distract the lad from removing

all his clothes. There was something naughty and schoolboyish about stripping in front of one of your friends, and James loved the idea of having the lad stand naked before him.

Gabriel looked timid and shy standing there with only his underpants on. They were made of white cotton, just like the ones James had masturbated over the previous night, but now the lad was giving his permission for him to look at them.

'Sorry. I'm a bit nervous about doing this, sir.' Gabriel swallowed and rubbed his hands uneasily against the sides of his bare legs. 'You see, it's just that I've never done this kind of thing before.'

'Well, you don't have to do it if you don't want to.' James tried to calm him.

'But do *you* want me to?'

'Of course I do,' James reassured him. 'I'd love to draw you with your clothes off.'

'All right then.' Gabriel placed his hands onto the band at the top of his underpants and lowered them ever so slightly, just enough for James to see the top of his pubic hair. 'Here goes then,' he said and pulled them right down.

The memories of the night before flooded back and James saw himself once again kneeling beside the bed sucking on the boy's cock. Gabriel had nothing to be shy about because James had seen it all before, and anyway he looked beautiful. He could not stop himself from staring longingly at the lad's fine, muscular figure, his thick, hairy legs and the ample penis that hung down in front of him. He had just the right mixture of boy and man in his physique. James looked down at his paper, not wanting to stare too much in case the lad became aware that there was more in his desire to draw him than just an artistic interest.

After a few moments of James trying to size up the boy in comparison to his piece of paper and put his figure in perspective, an idea occurred to him. Perhaps Gabriel could get himself into a better position. There was nothing particularly challeng-

ing about sketching him standing upright, James thought. It would be better if he lay on the bed.

'Gabriel, do you think you could sit on the bed,' James asked in his sweetest voice. 'Please,' he added.

'Yeah, if you want,' the lad replied, and he crossed the room and sat on the edge of the bed. James caught a glimpse of his bottom as he turned. It looked large and firm as it had done when he had secretly parted the cheeks and inserted his tongue into the soft pinkness within.

'Can you sit back a little and bring your legs up towards your chest?' Gabriel followed his instructions, raised his legs and rested his weight on his elbows. This was exactly how James had longed to see the lad. His cock and balls fell down in front of him and beneath them his arsehole was just visible. James could make out the inside of the lad's buttocks and the line of hair running the length of his perineum right down to the tight pink opening. 'That's fine.' A smile lit up Gabriel's face, and he looked, for the first time, a little relaxed.

James began to sketch, and as he did so, became more and more aware of how overpoweringly erotic the situation was. He felt that with every intense glance at the lad he was somehow violating him, invading his personal space. He was the voyeur, and Gabriel his willing subject. At the same time that his eyes devoured the boy's body, so his pencil seemed to touch and stroke every part of his model's skin and muscles. He lingered over the lad's upper arms, his thick waist, the pert nipples, and finally, the thick penis and weighty glands.

His own prick was now pushed upwards into a violent erection, and as he moved his pencil across the paper he realised that Gabriel too had the beginnings of a stiffening in his cock. It was almost imperceptible at first, but every time James looked up from his drawing the lad's penis had become a little harder. Obviously the feeling of being scrutinised by another boy was enough to arouse him. He did not look down, but his face twisted into an expression of guilt that James could not mistake.

By now Gabriel's cock was fully erect and James was almost panting with desire – the desire to reach out and grab the lad, take his prick and force it into his mouth. He could not help but stare deeply into the lad's eyes. Gabriel stared back. Without thinking further than his desperation to possess him, James leapt up, his sketch falling to the floor half finished, and he fell towards Gabriel and pushed his lips onto the lad's.

For what seemed like only a few seconds James felt a tongue slide into his mouth and Gabriel's lips push back onto his own. He did not dare to touch the boy, nor did he feel any hands upon him, but they kissed softly yet intensely for a beautiful moment.

'Look, I've got to go,' Gabriel panted, pulling his mouth away and getting up from the bed. James remained silent while the lad frantically gathered his clothes together, pulled them on and without another word left the room.

James wanted to go after him but did not dare. Instead he fell back on the bed and gazed breathlessly at the ceiling, not knowing quite what he should do. There was definitely reciprocation in Gabriel's kiss, but it was combined with a desire to hide or run away from his true feelings. James felt both elated by what liberation had occurred, but at the same time as if there was a matter that was far from resolved. He was determined to pursue the problem at the next possible opportunity.

After dinner Barnaby took James to one side in the hall and whispered to him that they should perhaps take a walk into the village. It was still quite bright outside even though it was almost eight o'clock in the evening. That was the beauty of a summer's night, thought James as they strode down to the village.

'So, what are you up to this time?' James asked with a tone of mock-suspicion. 'I'm beginning to get used to your little adventures now, and I think I know what they always lead to.'

'Aah, I can't keep anything from you, can I? You're too

clever for me.' The two boys laughed and walked on together until they reached the beginning of Rolvenden's main street.

'So where are we going?' said James, as they passed the little shop where Gabriel had bought some cigarettes on their first trip out together.

'To see the boys, of course.'

'Tom and Tank, you mean?' James asked.

'That's right. I said I was going to arrange a meeting at some point today.' James nodded. 'Well, I ran into them earlier and they said they'd be in the public house tonight.' Barnaby stopped speaking for a moment. 'So here we are,' and he gestured towards the New Queen's Head, the village's only pub.

The boys entered and Barnaby ordered drinks for the two of them. No sooner had he paid than James sighted Tom and Tank sitting in the corner of the room with two girls. 'They're over there,' James said, subtly indicating to his cousin.

'Well, in that case we'll have two more pints of cider,' he said, handing the money over to the barman. 'James, after you.' They made their way over to the table where the lads were sitting chatting to a couple of village girls. 'How are you boys?' Barnaby said in a confident tone, completely ignoring the women.

'We're fine, sir. Are those for us?' said Tom, pointing at the two glasses of cider. Barnaby handed them to the boys with a nod. 'Thank you. Isn't that kind of Mr Barnaby, Tank?' he said to his friend.

'Indeed it is.' Tank took hold of his pint and sipped with grateful zest.

'There's plenty more where they came from,' Barnaby added, with a wry smile.

'I'm sure there is,' said Tom under his breath, and the two lads gave one another a knowing look. 'So, what brings you in here?'

'We came looking for you boys, as well you know.' Barnaby

took a long drink from his glass before adding, 'We were planning a little private party back at the house, and we wondered whether you'd be interested in coming along?'

'Well, we were actually trying to win a favour or two with these girls,' Tom said in a whisper, gesturing towards the women who were now talking amongst themselves.

'Girls?' Barnaby sneered. 'You can chat to girls anytime. We've got lots of drink back at Sunningdale. I'm sure you'll have more fun with us.'

James stayed silent throughout this conversation, determined to let his cousin do the talking, just in case he said something stupid and ruined everything. The two village lads looked at one another and grinned. They turned to the girls and made their excuses.

Barnaby had arranged to have more furniture moved into the summer house along with four bottles of Sunningdale's finest champagne. It seemed like the perfect place for a secret meeting between village and estate boys.

James watched as Tom and Tank took cautious sips from their glasses.

'Not bad this stuff, is it?' said Tank. 'No wonder you lot drink so much of it.' Everyone laughed.

In addition to the chaise-longue, armchairs and table that had always been there, there was now a low bed, large enough for two people, and a simple wooden chair. Tom and Tank were seated in the easy chairs and James and his cousin sat side by side on the bed. They had managed to consume three of the four bottles of champagne and were by now all very drunk. In his haze of insobriety James's mind flipped back to the last time he was in the summer house at night, and the lovely image of Samuel Grainger with his clothes off. He looked across at the boys and wondered whether there would be a similar evening in store for him tonight. Tom and Tank, however, would be more difficult to seduce out of their clothes.

'Oh, yes, we're terribly good drinkers,' Barnaby said. 'Although that's about all the upper classes are any good at.'

'We're pretty good at drinking too,' said Tom. 'Amongst other things.'

'Well, I think you've been slightly unfair.' Barnaby paused as if to allow the lads time to ponder over his statement. James was puzzled.

'I don't quite catch your meaning, sir,' said Tom with a confused tone of voice.

'Both James and I have, at various points, enjoyed the pleasure of your company in the old barn down by the river.' Barnaby looked from one boy to the other as they sat in silence staring back at him. 'We've been welcomed into your gang, in the most –' he carefully searched for the word '– intriguing manner. Now perhaps it's time for us to stage our own initiation. What do you say, James?'

'Oh, yes, definitely,' he agreed, not knowing quite what his cousin was up to.

'That's if these young men want to be in *our* gang,' he added, throwing a questioning look at Tank and Tom.

'Yeah, of course we want to be in your gang,' said Tom. 'What do we have to do?'

'Oh, you're probably not man enough to take it,' Barnaby retorted.

'What do you mean, not man enough?' Tom turned to his friend. 'We're tough as anything, eh, Tank?'

'Too right! What do we have to do?' the lad enquired.

'Since you put us through our paces, so to speak, we're going to give you just as hard a time.' Barnaby stood up and walked over to the side of the bed. 'Do you think you can take it?'

'Of course we can,' Tom and Tank answered in unison.

'As you wish.' He crouched down and let his hand slide under the bed. When he brought his hand back out again it was grasping a long, thin piece of cane. He swished it through

the air making a cruel cutting noise. 'Stand up and keep your mouths shut, unless I tell you to speak.' The two lads glanced sideways at one another and then slowly got to their feet. 'That's right,' said Barnaby, lightly slapping the palm of his hand with the cane. 'We're going to see what you can take.' He walked towards the wooden chair and positioned it in the centre of the summer house. Then he took off his jacket and rolled up his sleeves. 'Right! You first,' he said, pointing his stick at Tom. 'Take off your coat, boy, and undo the top button of your breeches.' Slowly the lad did as he was commanded and, with a nervous look in his eyes like a guilty schoolboy awaiting punishment, he undid his breeches.

James watched in amazement at his cousin's expertise; it seemed as if he could have any boy that he wanted, a mere word being enough to trick them into some shameful act. He knew what would happen next and his prick stiffened. The very idea of having so much power over the manly boy made James quiver with excitement. He remembered the time he had been compelled to beat his fag when he was at school, and how much secret pleasure he had taken from the occasion. He prayed that Barnaby would allow him to join in with the game.

'Now bend over the chair,' his cousin ordered, and with his head bowed low in shame Tom, taking a frightened glance at the cane, leant across the back of the hard wooden piece of furniture. It was just the right height to allow him to bend over with his feet still just reaching the floor. Barnaby placed an authoritative hand on the back of the boy's breeches and gave them a sharp yank. They fell to the ground. Tom's shirt tails covered the seat of his underpants and Barnaby had to lift them up in order to slip the lad's underwear down and expose his firm buttocks.

James's cock twitched violently and he could feel his balls aching for release as he glimpsed the lad's rounded cheeks. However, it was a brief showing, as the shirt tails once again

covered them. Tom looked so vulnerable bent over the chair – an expression of distress on his face – with the hard back jabbing into his stomach. He gripped onto the sides and clenched his teeth, while Tank looked on in dread.

Barnaby stepped back to view the lad spread across the chair in front of him, and as he did so he let the cane once more whistle through the air in a frightening warning for what was to come. The boy who had once seemed so confident and virile was now reduced to a wimpering child awaiting punishment.

'So, are you ready for your caning?' Barnaby asked in a strict, schoolmaster tone of voice. Tom gave a nervous nod and closed his eyes. 'I want you to count out loud after every stroke. Do you understand?' The lad nodded again.

Barnaby took a step back from the chair and aimed the tip of his cane towards the place where the tails of Tom's shirt covered his buttocks. With a graceful flick he lifted back the lad's shirt and his fleshy arse cheeks were revealed for all to see. James felt so excited at the sight that he could barely control himself. He longed to be allowed to do what his cousin was doing, and hoped that he would be given a turn.

Barnaby lifted the cane into the air until it was above the level of his shoulder, and held it there for a moment before sending it flying down with a high-pitched whistling sound. It made a cruel-sounding slap on Tom's naked bottom, and the lad flinched in response and dug his fingers into the sides of the chair. 'One,' he counted in a wavering voice, trying not to show the pain of the whack. James knew, however, from experience that the first blow was always the most startling and painful, and left one feeling ashamed and violated.

His cousin stepped back so that everyone could see the red mark left by the first stroke and the boy's buttocks quivering from the impact of the blow. With a wicked look in his eyes Barnaby drove the cane down for the second time. This slap was even harder than the previous and Tom let out a yelp, like

that of a helpless child. 'Two.' It was as if he could barely even pronounce the word so painful was the feeling of Barnaby's beating.

These strokes were followed by four others, seeming each time to grow more vicious and cruel. Tom whimpered as each blow landed on his naked arse cheeks, but he gritted his teeth, gripped hard to the chair and counted the strokes of the cane. After the sixth whack Barnaby stopped and looked at the punished lad bent over the seat in front of him. His buttocks were marked with long red lines from where the cane had struck his fleshy cheeks. James imagined the smarting sensation Tom must now be feeling, and was impressed at how composed the lad had remained. He had not once begged for mercy nor had a tear escaped from the corner of his eye, as James was sure would be the case if such a severe beating had been given to him.

'That's it,' said Barnaby. 'You can get up now.' As the lad stood up James noticed the throbbing erection that stuck out in front of him and the shiny purple head that had stripped itself of its foreskin. The blows of the cane had clearly excited Tom and he quickly pulled up his trousers, not wanting the other boys to see how aroused he had become. As he did so he carefully rubbed his sore bottom and moved across to the edge of the room. He looked shamed and belittled, and James felt rather sorry for him. How the strong man can so easily fall, he thought to himself.

'Right,' Barnaby said, turning his attention to Tank. 'Your turn.' The lad looked so worried James was sure that at any moment he might burst into tears. 'James, would you like to administer the punishment this time?'

James's eyes lit up and he eagerly nodded his head in reply. This was the moment he had been hoping for, and he leapt from where he had been sitting on the corner of the bed and took hold of the cane that Barnaby held out to him. This was James's chance to play out his schoolboy fantasies with real-life

boys, and there was no possibility of unfavourable repercussions this time.

'Undo the buttons of your breeches,' James said in imitation of his cousin's authoritative commands. 'And take your jacket off.' Tank did as he was told. James, impatient and too excited by the situation to control himself, roughly pushed Tank across the back of the chair where moments earlier his friend had been caned. He then pulled the lad's trousers and underwear down to his ankles and flipped back the tails of his shirt. Tank's buttocks were larger and softer looking than Tom's, more like those of a young boy, and James felt a little sorry for them knowing as he did the beating they were about to receive.

Without any word of warning James raised the cane and brought it down with a crack onto the lad's exposed cheeks. Tank yelped with pain and James's cock twitched violently in his trousers. He had total power over the helpless lad before him and his strokes were cruel and hard, and left long marks across Tank's soft boyish cheeks. With every whack of the rod Tank sobbed louder and louder until he was eventually pleading for mercy.

'Sir, please stop,' he wailed and raised his head from its low position. 'Have I not been punished enough?' James had already given him ten strokes and Tank's rear was red with the lashings. He paused to take in the lad's pleas for mercy, then pushed his head back down and allowed another three harsh strokes to slap across the boy's arse.

'I think he's had enough now,' James said, turning to his cousin. 'What do you think?'

'Oh, yes, you've given him a good chastisement.' The two boys smiled at one another. 'Perhaps you should kiss it better for him now,' suggested Barnaby.

James knew exactly what his cousin was suggesting, and having his approval was enough to fill James with the confidence he needed. He instantly fell to his knees – so excited was he from giving the caning – and pushed his face towards Tank's

rotund arse. With a swift movement of his hands he gripped hold of the cheeks and prised them apart revealing the long strip of sensitive flesh between his buttocks. James paused for a moment, making sure that no objection came from the lad's lips or any movement from his body to suggest a desire to escape. Tank remained motionless, so James continued.

With great gusto he inhaled the sweet aroma from the lad's parted buttocks and let his finger slide down the sweat-drenched crack. The violence of his beating had made the boy perspire in panic, and the smell and feel of the droplets made James even more crazy to possess him completely – as a man possesses a woman. He attacked the musky crease with the extended probe of his tongue. Tank emitted a deep sigh of pleasure and James sank the tip of his tongue deeply into the puckered arsehole, which seemed to open with resignation. The saliva that ran in enthusiasm from his mouth added to the slippery nature of Tank's arse and allowed James the privilege of exploring even further into the lad's anal passage.

By now his cock was almost bursting and he knew that something would have to be done about it soon or else it would explode. Tank's open acceptance of James's intrusive tongue and his little pants of pleasure sanctioned further liberties, and James gleefully inserted two fingers into the wet opening that was the lad's arsehole. They slid in without any effort, and James could tell, even though the boy was most certainly a virgin, that it would not be difficult to penetrate the lad with something larger than just his fingers.

James rubbed his face all over Tank's buttocks in an attempt to soak up every inch of the beauty and softness of his bottom. He ached to be able to thrust his cock between those passive cheeks and open up the lad's slippery passageway, in the same way as he had been transgressed by Tom back in the old barn.

He then felt a tap on his shoulder. It was Barnaby. In his enthusiasm to taste Tank's most intimate zone he had quite forgotten the presence of Tom and his cousin. James stopped

what he was doing and turned around. The two boys were staring at him, a look of amazement on their faces. Barnaby seemed to know exactly how he was feeling and was clearly aroused by the display, judging from the bulge at the front of his trousers. He held out a hand containing the small jar of Vaseline that he had used the night before on Sam.

'Thanks,' James said in a breathless voice, and he stood up and began to unbutton his own breeches. The desire to insert his cock into Tank's arsehole was greater than his nervousness at being watched by the other boys, and he let his trembling penis spring out from its home. His breeches and underwear were pushed down so that the light breeze that passed through the summer house cooled his naked rear.

Tank turned around as if to catch a glimpse of what was to come next. 'Be gentle with me, sir,' he whispered. James gave him a short smile of reassurance and Tank returned to his submissive position with his head resting on the seat of the chair. James took this as evidence of the lad's willingness to be used as a source for his release, and he opened the jar and slicked his fingers with the lubricating grease. Returning the jar to Barnaby, James put some of the substance onto the head of his prick, the foreskin of which was pulled back to reveal his shiny purple helmet, and rubbed it all over and along the length of the thick shaft.

With the remaining lubricant on his fingers James proceeded to grease up Tank's arsehole. He slid his fingers around the rim of the tightly muscled entrance and into the deep, warm passage. Tank took in a deep breath, the coldness of the Vaseline probably shocking to his sensitive virginal parts – the places where boys were not supposed to be touched, and certainly never expected to find pleasure from.

James withdrew his fingers from the lad's arsehole and replaced them with the tip of his cock. The swollen head slipped into the opening without any trouble and James rested it there for a moment. He wanted to savour the occasion – it

would be the first time he had ventured so far with another boy. Then, as Tank's muscles began to relax again after the shock of the initial intrusion, he gave a firm thrust of his hips and drove the rest of his member deeply into the lad's arse.

Tank let out a cry that sounded more in shock at James's sudden penetration than in actual pain. This did not deter James; the feeling was so overpowering that he could not have withdrawn even if his life depended on it. The lad's passage felt warm and tight, clamped as it was around his rock-hard prick. James remained motionless for a moment in order to allow both himself and Tank to adjust to the situation. Soon, however, he could feel the tight muscles loosening as they began to welcome the intrusion of his organ.

James started to thrust his hips backwards and forwards, the Vaseline making his movements smooth and deep. He pulled his prick back until it was almost completely out of the lad's arse and then thrust it violently back inside, making Tank gasp with the shock of the re-entry. It felt hot and slippery inside the boy and James wanted to remain in there for ever, as each rhythmic movement of his prick sent a shudder through his whole body. Suddenly he realised why the two lads had been so eager to penetrate him – the feeling was magnificent.

While he was shoving his penis in and out of the lad, James noticed out the corner of his eye his cousin moving around the side of the chair. He approached Tank, whose face was at the same level as his crotch, and ran his fingers through the lad's hair. Then, with an experienced hand he slipped his breeches down and unbuttoned his underpants. James could not believe the size of his cousin's erection. His cock was long and uncircumcised, with thick veins running down its length. At the very tip there glistened a clear droplet of sticky fluid – the precursor of desire.

Without a word Tank reached out and grasped Barnaby's balls as they hung before him. He had a hungry look in his eyes and as he caressed the heavy glands Barnaby put a hand on the

back of his head and moved his stiff cock closer to the lad's face. Tank opened his mouth and the huge member slipped inside. James had a perfect view of the boys. He could see the look of pleasure on his cousin's face as his cock slid in and out of the boy's mouth. It was good that Tank had such big lips and so wide a mouth or he would never have been able to accommodate all of the penis.

'How is he at that end?' Barnaby asked with a cheeky grin.

'Very nice,' said James. 'Very tight.'

'He has expert lips, I must say.'

James continued to make love to Tank from behind while his cousin filled the lad's other orifice. He could not speak, but simply serve to pleasure the two boys. A feeling of total ecstasy began to mount up in James's loins and he thought that he might spurt at any moment, when suddenly he felt the gentle touch of fingers on his naked arse. It was Tom. The display of lust was clearly too much for him and he wanted to join in.

James slowed down his thrusting movements and bent his body forward a little to allow Tom as much access as possible to his backside. The lad's hands drifted over the small of his back and down onto his buttocks, which tensed spontaneously when touched. James could feel fingers creeping closer to his hidden recesses – the parts that the same lad had so roughly examined in the barn. This time, however, they were tender in their caresses. Tom's fingers parted James's arse cheeks and began to probe into his anal opening. He could feel the digits slide inside, lubricated with saliva probably, and push hard against his prostate, which made his prick tingle even more. Then the fingers were withdrawn and James felt, for the first time in his life, the thrill of another boy's tongue coming into contact with his sensitive ring.

The sensation of Tom's tongue delving into and around his arsehole, coupled with the powerful stimulation of Tank's warm little bottom contracted about his cock, was enough to

almost make James pass out. The feeling of ecstasy was overwhelming and he felt dizzy with the pleasure of it all.

After a while Tom ceased his anal probing and pulled his face away from where James had felt its presence at his rear. He wondered what the boy was up to, but did not turn around in case it distracted him. Also the sight of Tank sucking away at his cousin's cock was far too enjoyable viewing to look away from.

The next thing James was aware of was something hard and slippery being pushed between his buttocks. He could feel the tip of Tom's warm knob pushing into his already saliva-drenched hole. It was a lovely sensation, for this time the thrill of his own cock working away inside Tank made him more relaxed and open to its intrusion. The lad's member seemed to glide into him, almost without the slightest feeling of discomfort, only a powerful shudder of fulfilment running through his body.

James gasped as Tom pushed himself inside right up to the hilt. He could feel soft pubic hairs tickling the sides of his arse cheeks, and the lad's stomach as it pushed against his lower back. The cock was thrusting in and out, making James gasp in rapture. When it was pushed fully in it touched against his prostate and this increased the aching desire in his balls to relieve themselves.

All four boys were by this point panting furiously and it was clear that they were nearing their orgasms. James could feel the pounding of Tom's cock in his arse becoming overpoweringly stimulating and his cock stiffened inside Tank like it never had before in his life.

All of a sudden Barnaby released a long, hoarse sigh and he reached out and gripped tightly onto Tank's head, holding it firmly in place. James could tell that he was ejaculating a large helping of spunk into the lad's mouth. Tank looked as if he were desperate to lap up as much of it as possible and sucked with verve at the long organ.

The lad's passage was still milking frantically at his prick, and it had by now grown intense enough to bring James to a convulsive climax. The pressing feeling at the base of his cock, edged on by Tom's thrusting motions from behind, took him over and a torrent of semen pushed itself up the shaft and came bursting out of the tip and into the lad before him. The pleasure was so intense that James could barely breathe. His whole being was concentrated on his climax and the thought of filling the lad with his seed. He let out a yelp and gripped onto Tank's breast with one hand. With the other he instinctually reached down and clutched the boy's furry balls. This was clearly enough stimulation to bring Tank off, and James felt the boy shudder in his arms and a warm jet of fluid shot out across his hand and the back of the chair.

At the same time, from behind, there came the inevitable grunts obviously driven out of Tom by the potency of his own orgasm. James could feel him holding tightly onto his shoulders and pushing his cock inside as far as it would go. There was a shiver from his body and then the trickling sensation of the lad's sperm flowing from him and into James's passage. The sticky fluid seeped out of him and ran down the back of his leg. He felt Tom pull himself free and sigh − a long sigh that sounded as if it were filled with a mixture of forbidden pleasure and fulfilled desire.

The four boys stood still for a short while spent and exhausted. Barnaby grinned his inimitable smile and for a brief second James caught his eye and they exchanged a look of common understanding − the emotion a boy feels after orgasm and before continuing with everyday life.

Tom and Tank, not even bothering to wipe themselves clean, slipped back into their clothes and said their goodbyes. 'Does this mean we're in the gang now?' Tom asked.

'Oh, I should say so,' Barnaby smiled. 'What do you think, James old boy?'

'Absolutely,' he managed in an exhausted tone.

The lads picked up their jackets, made a vain attempt to tidy their ruffled hair and left the summer house. Barnaby sat down on the bed, poured himself a final glass of champagne and closed his eyes. 'Dear me, those boys really know how to enjoy themselves.'

Seven

'Dear Mother,' wrote James, 'I am having a splendid time. The Compton-Crofts have made me feel very welcome and there have been no troubles at all. The house is lovely, but the countryside is even better. It's the perfect place to paint and draw. I'm in my element. Barnaby is such fun. I shall be very sad to have to return, even though I miss you, of course.' He put his pen down for a moment and pondered what to write next. The problem was that most of the really exciting things that had happened he would never be able to tell his mother. How James longed to explain all about Samuel Grainger, the village boys and his adoration of Gabriel – but he never could.

It was Gabriel's day off and he wondered where the beautiful youth might be. Lying in bed? Relaxing by the river? Probably with his girl, thought James. He did not understand how someone so lovely could be wasted on a woman. Why could he not possess him totally? The thought of his shapely body and full, rounded bottom gave James a heavenly sensation in his groin, and he thought hard for a plan to gain the boy's love. The kiss they had shared two days ago seemed so significant and revealing of Gabriel's true feelings and James wondered

whether the lad was simply too shy or afraid to let out his real emotions.

The memory of the lad's cock sliding in and out of his mouth gave James a sickness in his stomach; a sense of shame for having been forced to steal the moment from Gabriel without his consent or even his knowledge.

James decided that he should take the opportunity of the lad's day off and seek him out. Yes, that was it. He would find Gabriel and suggest a picnic in the woods. He could bring sandwiches and cake and perhaps even some wine. He did not know whether the boy drank wine, but the champagne had seemed to work so well with Tom and Tank that perhaps it would have the same effect on Gabriel. Alcohol was the key to relaxing a lad enough so as to allow his natural instincts to take their proper course. It had helped to seduce the village boys into Barnaby's mischievous games, and that was good enough for James.

While he was thinking through his plan and wondering what the best time and place to look for the lad would be, the door of his bedroom burst open and in strode his cousin.

'I hope I'm not disturbing you,' he began, 'but I thought I'd just mention the football match. Did my mother tell you?'

'No,' said James. 'What football match?'

'Ah, well, there's some strange old tradition in this part of the country that they hold a game of football for the village boys,' Barnaby explained.

'But it's not the season for football.' James looked confused.

'I know, but down here they like to kick off the season early. And anyway it keeps the locals happy.'

'Who's it played between?'

'The lads from Rolvenden and the Fryhurst boys,' said Barnaby. 'It's the nearest village to this one.'

'Ah, I see,' James said. 'When's it happening?'

'Saturday. Do come along so that we can cheer our boys on.' Barnaby moved towards the door as he was about to leave.

'Barnaby.' James halted his cousin as he was turning the handle. 'Will Gabriel be playing?' he enquired coyly.

Barnaby smirked and let out a barely audible laugh. 'Oh, James, you only ever think of one thing. Of course he'll be. He's our best player.' And with that he closed the door and left James alone in his room.

It was a lovely day as James cut a path through the grounds of Sunningdale and into the village. He was determined to find Gabriel and persuade him to come out for a picnic with him. But where would he be? James thought that he'd try the most likely place – down by the river.

He cut through the village, out past the station and into the surrounding country. At first glance across the open meadow that acted as one bank of the river there seemed to be nobody about, but as James drew closer to the scene he saw a figure bobbing about in the water. It was Gabriel.

When he caught sight of James standing watching him he stopped swimming and rested, clinging onto the riverbank.

'Hello,' said James.

'Hello, sir. I didn't expect to see you down here today.' His voice had a slightly distant tone to it. James was worried that by kissing him in his room as he had done, he had frightened him off, and maybe Gabriel would not want to be friends with him any more.

'I came looking for you. I thought you might be with your girl.'

'Well, there's a sorry tale in that,' said Gabriel with a sadness in his voice. 'We've had a bit of a falling-out, I'm afraid.'

'Oh, that's a shame,' said James, not intending it to be quite as sincere as it sounded. 'Perhaps I can cheer you up.' Gabriel looked up at him with the beginnings of a smile on his face. He looked terribly handsome standing there waist-deep in water, his torso shimmering in the afternoon sunshine and water dripping from his face and hair. 'I wondered whether a

145

little later on today you'd like to come on a picnic with me?'
There was a horrible moment of silence before the lad
answered. It was as if he needed to debate the whole situation
in his head before giving a decision.

'Yes. Why not? That sounds like a good idea,' he said.
'Although I don't have very much money for food or drink –'

'Don't worry about that,' James interrupted. 'I'll sort it out.
My aunt has plenty of food *and* money. I'll get something
organised.'

'All right. Shall we say four o'clock at the gatepost at the
back of the house?'

'That's fine,' replied James. 'Then we can decide where to
go from there.' He waved to his friend and turned around,
eager to make his way back to Sunningdale and prepare for the
picnic.

'Goodbye,' Gabriel called out as he galloped over the field.

'Goodbye,' James shouted back.

Lady Compton-Croft had said that she would make the
arrangements with the kitchen staff so that a picnic hamper
could be put together. James asked whether he might have
champagne and beer, wanting to make sure that Gabriel would
have something to drink that he liked. He could collect the
food at three-thirty and still be in plenty of time to meet his
friend.

James grinned smugly to himself as he crossed through the
walled garden at the back of the house, hamper in hand, and
out towards the gate. When he got there Gabriel had not yet
arrived and he spent the next five minutes worrying that
perhaps the boy would not show. However, at just past four
o'clock, he heard a crunching of gravel underfoot and saw the
smiling face of the boy he loved.

It was decided that they should not go far, just into the
woods that lay behind Sunningdale. There they found a clearing
amongst the trees and laid down the tartan picnic cloth and

unpacked the hamper. James took a certain secret pleasure from the look of excitement on Gabriel's face as he saw all the splendid food that had been prepared for them. He knew that the lad came from a poor background and could never have afforded the luxuries that James had become used to. It gave him a pleasing feeling to be able to share his good fortune with those less lucky than himself, and secretly he hoped that it would also make Gabriel feel relaxed enough to allow James to seduce him.

Even though the boys were surrounded by trees, a clear summer light shone through the gaps between the branches and lit the clearing where they sat cross-legged on the warm ground. The sun was still high in the sky and they basked in its rays.

'These are nice sandwiches,' Gabriel mumbled in between mouthfuls.

'Which ones are you eating?'

'The salmon and cucumber ones.' He smiled and took another bite. James was happy to see the lad content and comfortable. It seemed as if the incident in his bedroom of two days ago was not a problem, or at least had been forgotten, and there was still a chance of persuading Gabriel into some more of the same.

The boys ate the food and drank the champagne and beer. They chatted about their lives and their plans for the future. And even though they had completely opposing backgrounds and lifestyles, they were still able to meet on common ground and share some everyday views. Three hours passed by extremely quickly and soon the sun was not so high in the sky, nor the woods so brightly lit and the area where they sat seemed a little cooler.

'Are you going to come and watch the football at the weekend?' Gabriel asked.

'Yes, of course,' James replied. 'Barnaby was telling me about it only this morning.'

'I'm really looking forward to it. I love football,' he added.

'I can't wait to see you play.' The thought of Gabriel in tight little shorts and long socks made James feel extremely aroused, and he fought with himself for a moment to control the beginnings of an erection.

The boys sat back on the ground together in silence. James glanced across at Gabriel every now and again to check what he was doing and also to take a look at that lovely face that never ceased to please him. The lad looked so calm and at peace with himself that James did not want to spoil the moment with words. However, after a while he could not resist asking a question.

'What are you thinking about?' he said, sitting up a little in order to gain the lad's attention.

'I was just thinking about the other day in your room.' James's heart leapt into his throat, wondering what Gabriel would say next. 'I'm sorry I ran out like I did, sir.'

'That's all right,' James cautiously replied.

'It's not that I minded you kissing me,' he paused for a moment as if collecting his thoughts, 'in fact it was quite nice.' James's heart leapt once again, but this time for joy. He could barely believe what he was hearing. Gabriel kept his eyes focused on the ground while he spoke. 'I'm just a bit shy, that's all, sir, and it took me rather by surprise.'

Gabriel fell silent again and James, not wanting to question him further for fear of being told something he did not want to hear, allowed the subject to drop. This was enough to boost his confidence and give him the strength to be a little more bold in future.

'Sir?'

'Yes?' replied James.

'Would you do me a favour?'

'What?' James could not imagine what he could ever do that would be of use to Gabriel, but he enquired none the less.

'Would you massage my shoulders? They aren't half aching,'

he said. And without waiting for a response, he sat up and turned around where he was sitting so that his back was facing James.

'Of course,' he replied. 'And I wish you'd stop calling me sir.'

'Sorry.'

James felt terribly excited to be actually asked to touch the lad, and with cautious hands he reached forward and took hold of his shoulders. He felt liberated by the drink they had been consuming throughout the afternoon and hoped that Gabriel would feel the same. Gently he massaged the lad's shoulders. They felt hard and tense and James could locate each muscle beneath the skin. The lad let out a groan of pleasure and he rubbed a little harder.

'Hold on,' said Gabriel. 'If I take this off it'll be easier.' And without hesitation he unbuttoned his shirt and let it fall from his shoulders. His back was broad and strong-looking, wide at the top and gradually sloping down towards a slender waist. James recommenced his massage, but this time not hindered by Gabriel's clothing. He let his hands wander across the lad's back and shoulders, with care stroking every inch of his smooth skin. The flesh felt soft and warm, and as he touched its surface James could feel his penis stiffening in his trousers.

'Is that all right?' he asked.

'Lovely,' Gabriel said in a trance of pleasure, like a dog having his tummy tickled.

As he rubbed the lad's back an idea came into James's head. 'Lie down,' he said with a confidence even Barnaby would have been proud of. 'On your back.' Gabriel did as he was told without so much as the slightest questioning look. James began to work on the lad's stomach and upper body. He let his hands run across the smooth, taut flesh and over his fully developed pectorals. The skin felt stretched and soft and he slowly massaged until he could hear the lad's breath quickening. The further his hands seemed to travel down Gabriel's stomach the more heavily he breathed.

149

James soon began to concentrate his strokes on the lad's hardened stomach. He loved the soft patch of dark hair that encircled his navel then ran downwards towards the waistband of his breeches. James hoped that Gabriel would allow him to venture down there, and he rubbed away to the sound of the boy's purring response.

Looking up at his friend, James noticed that the lad's eyes were closed and he had put his arms behind his head to act as a pillow against the wood's harsh ground. Also, as he glanced down at Gabriel's crotch he noticed a distinct bulge forming in his heavy canvas breeches. A little tingle of delight vibrated through James's body at the sight of his companion's obvious excitement. It was as if he had the power, with a touch of his hands, to bring to life the lad's most hidden feelings and desires. Just like William, the boy he had manually seduced in Rosendale Park, he had Gabriel exactly where he wanted him – a victim of the flesh.

With the utmost care James began to unbutton the top of Gabriel's breeches. There was no sign of objection from the lad so James continued until they were fully undone. By this time he could see the top of a pair of clean white underpants with small fasteners down the front, and beneath them an impressive bulge. From the top of the lad's underwear a delicate covering of fine pubic hair sprouted forth through which James carefully ran his fingers.

James pulled the lad's breeches a little lower down his legs in order to more fully expose the cotton underwear. He leant forward a fraction, trying not to be seen by Gabriel, and took a sniff. The boy smelt fresh and cleanly washed with just the slightest hint of sweat and bodily odour, exactly the same as those James had smelt the night he'd sneaked into the lad's room. He inhaled deeply the sweet smell of his secret areas. This time, however, his invasions were sanctioned.

Gabriel took in a sharp breath and thrust his crotch forward provocatively, as if to encourage James's attentions. The bulge

had now become the outline of a fully erect penis. With the most delicate touch James stroked along the contours of the hard shape. His own prick pulsated violently in his breeches and he yearned for the opportunity to relieve himself.

The pleasure derived from touching Gabriel's erection was too intense and James withdrew his hand. He had decided that it would now be possible to use his mouth and calmly pressed his lips to the lad's stomach. The flesh felt warm and solid and he let his tongue slip out and over the skin, tasting Gabriel's saltiness.

James was soon drawn to the hard little nipples that poked out of his chest. He took one into his mouth and ran his tongue around the edge and across its stiff tip. It seemed to harden in his mouth, and the saliva he dribbled onto it made it possible for him to caress the purple tit with his fingers as he once again moved his mouth further down Gabriel's chest.

The lad's prick looked harder than ever in his tight cotton underpants and James softly kissed the place where it lay concealed. There came no word of objection from the boy, only a slight groan of entreaty. James took his cue and slowly unbuttoned Gabriel's underwear until it fell open and revealed his rock-hard prick jutting upwards long and thick. It was just like that night he had pleasured the sleeping boy.

He pushed his face close to the erection before him and inhaled its clean, boyish smell. He could not stop himself from taking the head into his mouth and gently sucking it. Gabriel let out a long, low moan of pleasure, and James, with his head resting against the lad's tensed stomach, allowed the penis to glide all the way into his wet mouth. It tasted of soap and water, with the slightest hint of Gabriel's own special musk. He took hold of the boy's heavy, furry balls that hung beneath the straining erection thrusting like a length of steel into his mouth, and squeezed them in the palm of his hand.

James stretched out his body on the ground so as to have maximum access to Gabriel's cock, with his feet pointing

towards the boy's head and his face buried in his crotch. He let his tongue and lips run up and down the length of the penis, while his free hand wanked the shaft from the bottom, thus providing additional stimulation.

All of a sudden James felt something touching his own penis, which throbbed within his trousers. He could sense Gabriel's hand as it began to undo his breeches and underwear and he felt what he had for so long dreamed about – the beautiful lad's mouth around the head of his penis.

Both boys were lying on their sides sucking one another's cocks. The awkward position they were in was enough to force their erect shafts down the other's throat and they greedily lapped away. James could taste the fluid that trickled from the end of Gabriel's, and it left a salty flavour at the back of his throat. With one hand gripping tightly onto the hefty glands, James used the other to push down the lad's underpants far enough to gain access to his soft arse cheeks. Gabriel exhaled a grunt of gratification in between mouthfuls and James felt dissolved with the pleasure of the lad's lips clamped tightly about his penis.

He let his hand glide over the lad's smooth buttocks until he could feel, for the first time, their rhythmic thrusting, edging their owner's cock further into his mouth. James moved his fingers towards the crevice between the two muscular cheeks and met with Gabriel's warm, sweaty arse crack. He moved the tips of his fingers along the groove and allowed them to rest on the tight little hole that led into the boy. James recalled the night he had gently parted his sleeping friend's bottom cheeks and explored that secret cavity with his fingers and tongue. Now he let the tip of one digit dip into the warm, tight ring, and he felt the lad's balls tighten beneath his grasp. The hole was muscled and wet with sweat. James inserted a second finger alongside the first in order to widen the opening and increase Gabriel's feeling of ecstasy when he eventually spilt his seed.

James continued to suck the cock that pushed forth into his

mouth and the sensation produced by his lips over the stiff shaft seemed to relax Gabriel, and his arsehole loosened slightly. He began to move the fingers that were slotted up inside the lad, firstly bringing them out, then shoving them back inside, and finally twisting them about. It felt tight and moist inside Gabriel and James let his fingers stay there, pushed as far in as was possible.

Gabriel followed his example and James's breath was taken away by the sudden sensation of two cold fingers probing around his arsehole. Before he could even register their presence they were rammed into him and it felt as if his cock would burst at any moment. They seemed to instantly intensify the feelings that ran through his body in waves. He knew that it would not be possible to hold in the impending explosion any longer and as he surrendered to his body's natural pattern so there came, as if in sympathy, a deep groan from Gabriel's direction.

James sucked madly, like his life depended on it, and at the same time as he felt himself spill into his companion's mouth so the lad's prick also began to spurt. Gabriel's cock was deep inside his mouth and the semen flooded the back of his throat with its lovely salty flavour. James drank down the jet of creamy liquid and teased the swollen head with his tongue. The sensation of Gabriel's mouth around his own shooting cock made James quiver with excitement and he wanted to swallow even more of the lad's discharge.

He could feel his own orgasm subsiding and the spurts of spunk from Gabriel also decreased until they were nothing more than a series of short trickles running out of his penis's very tip. The lads rolled onto their backs panting from the thrill of making one another spend. James still had some of Gabriel's semen in his mouth and he savoured the taste and texture of the liquid.

No one dared to say a word, both boys having gone further than they would ever have thought possible. James, however,

could not help a smile lighting up the corners of his mouth; Gabriel was beginning to show feelings for him that he would have thought impossible only days before. Perhaps he did care for him more than just as a friend. They may have indulged one another sexually, as boys often do in the absence of women, but this seemed a little too much. Gabriel must have even swallowed his come, thought James. That could only be a sign that there was more to his participation in their games than just a boyish lust for release.

'That wasn't supposed to happen, sir,' said Gabriel. His voice was quiet and low, sounding half in shame at what they had done and half still out of breath from the exertion of his orgasm.

'I know,' replied James, trying hard to sound as if he were ashamed of what they had done. 'But sometimes these things just happen.' Gabriel nodded and pulled his breeches back on.

'I must say, sir, even though it don't seem right, us being both boys and all,' he drew in a deep breath before continuing, 'but you're certainly better at it than any girl I've ever known.'

James beamed with pride at Gabriel's last comment, buttoned up his own breeches and got to his feet. He gathered the picnic things and carefully repacked the hamper.

'Will I see you at the match tomorrow?' Gabriel asked.

'Oh, yes. Absolutely,' replied James, and he watched as the lad waved a hand and walked off into the early evening's fading light.

Eight

The breakfast table looked even more full than usual. Lady Compton-Croft had requested every possible type of fruit and cereal, as well as eggs, bacon, sausages, tomatoes, mushrooms and smoked haddock. James felt hungry. Staying out so late with Gabriel had meant that he'd missed dinner and had to make do with some left-overs that the housekeeper had heated up for him.

'James? Some more eggs?' his aunt asked. 'After all, it'll be a long day. And no one enjoys themselves on an empty stomach.' She watched as James piled some more scrambled egg onto his plate and filled his tea cup.

'I thought that we might start out early,' said Barnaby. 'Get a head start and wish our boys good luck.' He turned to James. 'What do you think?'

'Oh, I see,' interrupted his mother. 'So you won't be travelling there in the motor with us?'

'No. I don't think so.' Barnaby looked at James, still waiting for his answer. 'Well?'

'Yes. Why not?' said James. 'They'd appreciate that.'

The football was due to begin at midday, but James agreed

that it would be nice to wish Gabriel luck before they started and also to have a private moment with him. They could see the boys beforehand and then join the rest of the family before the game began.

Barnaby and James excused themselves from the table and went upstairs to fetch their coats. When they were dressed and ready to go they wished Lady Compton-Croft a pleasant morning and set out down the main path.

The football pitch was located at the other end of Rolvenden, in a field just beyond where the river passed by the deserted barn. They walked with hands in pockets, James now very used to the journey from Sunningdale to the old barn. As they passed the site where the village lads would usually swim and play both young men looked longingly into the river as if there were memories trapped there – memories that seemed so vivid it was as if they could be glimpsed in the water's reflective surface.

They passed down a narrow path that ran along the river's edge, with water on one side and a copse on the other. There was a stile and beyond that three or four large open fields. This was where the match would take place. The pitch had been partitioned with iron posts and thick lengths of rope. At the far side there were rows of chairs and tables and at either side of the field were two small brick buildings that looked like elaborate privies.

'Those must be the changing rooms,' said Barnaby after a long silence. 'One for each team.'

'They don't look very big.' As James spoke there came footsteps in the bracken from behind and the cousins turned around to see who it was.

'What are you doing here so early?' said Tom.

'Hello,' Barnaby said in a pleasantly shocked tone. 'We thought we'd get here early and wish you boys luck before you got changed.'

Tom was accompanied by Tank and another boy. They all

had canvas bags slung across their shoulders and a confident look in their eyes. It was a warm morning and none of them were wearing jackets. They all had on the thinnest cotton shirts with the collars open and sleeves rolled up.

'I don't think you know Charlie,' said Tom, gesturing towards the third lad. James and Barnaby shook his hand.

'Pleased to meet you, sir,' Charlie said in a shy voice.

'I'm sure we must have seen you before with the lads,' James said, recalling his first meeting with Tom and Tank down by the river.

Charlie was slim and more delicate-looking than the other two, with fine blond hair and a small boyish frame. His exposed arms looked skinny and pale, but there was an innocent beauty in his clear blue eyes and soft lips.

'Shall we go and see what's happening with the preparations?' asked Tank.

'Yeah, why not,' said Tom and all five boys began to walk in the direction of the seats. There was a group of people standing around with boxes and balls and bottles of water, and Barnaby, being the only representative of the house, made their acquaintance. There were several young people from the village who had come along to offer their support and they knew the boys already. Also there were some older men and women, one of whom was the referee, and the others were there to help with the organisation and provide the lunch-time refreshments.

The three village lads were directed towards one of the brick buildings and told that this was to be the Rolvenden team's changing room. They picked up their bags and cut a path towards the building.

'You can come and talk to us while we get ready if you like,' said Tom.

'All right,' replied Barnaby. 'You coming, James?' He nodded and followed on behind the other boys.

The changing room was small and damp. It would have been

157

cramped with all eleven players inside, but on arrival they discovered that they were the first and so had more room to spread out. Two wooden benches ran the length of the room and there were hooks on the walls for the boys to hang their clothes on. In the corner was a shower large enough for two or three people to wash in at once.

'We've got here a bit early I think,' said Tank, slinging his bag onto one of the benches and starting to unlace his boots.

'Well, it's only half past ten,' Barnaby added looking at his pocket watch. 'The game doesn't start for ages.' He sat down next to Tank and crossed his legs. There was a moment of total silence which Barnaby disturbed. 'So are you boys going to get changed or not?'

Tom and Tank turned to one another as if they might find the answer concealed somewhere on the other's face. 'I suppose so,' Tom replied at last, and the village boys began to unpack their bags. James stood with his back to the door watching as each boy arranged his football kit and started to unbutton his shirt.

The lads stripped off their daytime clothes and hung them on the hooks provided. James marvelled at how fit and muscular their bodies looked; soft and boyish, yet at the same time hardening into the angular shape of a man. Their legs were covered with fine hairs that became thicker as they reached the tops of each boy's thick thighs. Tom and Tank especially looked more splendid than James remembered from their earlier encounters.

All three boys now stood naked except for their tight underwear, which clung close to their bodies, leaving little to the imagination. James was overpowered by how erotic the situation seemed – in the changing room with such beautiful boys in a state of undress. It was like being back at school.

'Hold on a second,' said Barnaby. They were about to pull down their underpants and get dressed for the match, but the

authoritative tone of his voice made them stop and stand quite still.

'What?' asked Tom. The bulge at the front of his underwear held James's attention, and he yearned to undress the boy fully and caress the treasures that lay beneath the heavy cotton.

'We've a little while before the game's set to start.' Barnaby turned to James. 'Can you lock the door, please?' James swivelled round and turned the huge key that stuck out from its rusty lock. The boys remained silent. 'You lads need to relax before the match if you want to win. And James and I are the perfect ones to offer our assistance to you.' He took off his jacket and hung it onto a peg. 'Now bend over the bench and we'll massage all that pre-soccer tension out of you.'

The lads looked at each other, and without a word Tom took the lead and laid himself forward across the bench so that his feet and hands were resting on the floor and the only part of him touching the wood was his groin. Tank and Charlie followed his example and positioned themselves alongside their friend.

They had the three boys at their disposal. James's prick throbbed violently and he looked forward to soon being able to find a release in the boys. It was like a sweet shop – too many treats to choose from.

'Can I take Tom first?' James asked. 'I haven't had a go with him before.'

'Very well,' agreed his cousin. 'And I'll start with Tank. We can both share Charlie.' The third boy was conveniently situated in the middle, allowing for easy access to him in between their dalliances with the other two.

James moved towards Tom and stood between his parted legs. He fell to his knees and pushed the lad's thighs as far apart as he could. James now had total access to the cotton-clad tensed buttocks that jutted upward in front of him. His hands stretched out and he let them drift gently over the small of Tom's back and his hairy thighs. His body felt warm and soft

159

and James could not resist lowering his face towards the lad's bottom and taking a little sniff. Twice he had been penetrated by him – the heavy buttocks using the fullness of their thrust to drive his prick deeply into James – but never had he explored the cheeks or tasted their inner flavour. The aroma that filled his nostrils was so pungent that James felt faint with aggressive desire. He knew immediately from the musky stench that he would have no alternative but to slip down the lad's underpants, pry the globes of flesh apart and dive inside.

James pulled down the material and the shape that had been suggested in its folds became reality. Two tensed buttocks presented themselves in all the glory of their nakedness. He once again inhaled their smell, more sweaty and masculine this time, without the cotton covering. James ran his hands over their smooth surface and then carefully moved them apart to reveal the secret groove between the cheeks. There was a line of fine dark hair running the length of Tom's crack which circled the pouting ring of his arsehole and carried on down over his perineum. James put his mouth close to the opening and dabbed his tongue into it. The lad let out a little whimper of pleasure and the muscles in his buttocks tensed even more.

The hole itself was tight and tasted salty from sweat and Tom's own bodily flavour. James let his tongue slip as far inside as was possible and then out again and over the rim. The lad wriggled but James held him firmly in place with a hand spreading each arse cheek. As he kissed and licked the dilating hole his nose came directly into contact with the rest of the lad's crease, and he was free to inhale the intense aroma secreted between the tightly confined buttocks. James thought about how they had been cooped up all day in the boy's underwear, rubbing against one another and producing their own lovely musk.

As James put his tongue to work he noticed out of the corner of his eye his cousin who was also employed in the same activity. It was Tank's arse, however, that was the object of his

attentions. James watched as he held the lad's arse cheeks apart and forcefully pushed his face between them. Charlie had not been forgotten either. Barnaby's unoccupied hand was down the back of the youth's underpants, and one of his fingers was working its way up his arsehole.

James felt he was becoming acquainted with Tom's bottom, but his cock and balls were still uncharted territory. Certainly they had been thrust into his face in the old barn, but now he was in control of the situation he wanted to explore them in his own time, using his own methods.

'Turn over,' he whispered into the boy's ear.

'All right, sir,' Tom replied. 'If you wish.' He raised himself, turned around and sat down on the bench facing James. His underpants were lowered at the back, but at the front they were still covering a straining erection.

Without another word James reached forward and dragged down the lad's underwear and took a hold of his thick jutting member. He felt fuelled with desire and could not stop himself from immediately drawing back the foreskin and plunging the cock into his mouth. The musky aroma left where the skin had concealed the bulbous head tasted heavenly, and James ran his tongue all over the swollen purple knob and probed the winking eye at the end.

Tom's balls were tight and hairy and James squeezed them in his clammy hand which sent a perceptible shudder through the boy's body. He continued to suck at the whole length of the penis, sometimes using his lips to stimulate the very tip and at other times allowing the organ to slide right to the back of his throat. James could taste the bitter trickle of pre-come which he knew to be a sign of Tom's enjoyment and imminent release.

James added to the lad's pleasure by slipping a finger into his muscled hole which had been relaxed a little from his finger-work earlier. Tom began to pant and moan and move his hips rhythmically, pushing his prick deeper into James's mouth.

Then came the moment of triumph and he felt a hot jet of spunk shoot from the tip of the boy's cock and onto his tongue. It was gulped down with verve and so were the other following streams of semen that pumped out. James sucked frantically, not wanting a single drop to be wasted. There was so much come that he was unable to swallow it all and it gathered in his mouth.

He stopped ejaculating and James, driven by an insatiable desire to gain access to every orifice of the lad's body, sat up on his haunches and kissed Tom full on the lips. Their mouths opened and the semen leaked from James's and into his companion's. He felt elated to be able to share the load with the one who had released it. The two boys remained pressed together for some moments before Tom pulled away panting breathlessly.

James glanced across at his cousin who seemed to have been performing the same act as him on Tank. Saliva dribbled down his chin from where he had been so concentrated on sucking the boy. He licked his lips in order to consume the last droplets of semen left around them.

'How's it going with you?' asked James.

'Very well. This lad is certainly easy to excite,' said Barnaby. 'And there's plenty of it in him.' He gave a cheeky grin and returned his attention to Tank's body. James noticed that Charlie was sitting on the bench looking a little dejected. Barnaby was so wrapped up in his boy that he had completely forgotten about the other lad.

James was still so sexually excited that he felt it would not be possible to cease their activities so soon. He knew exactly what he wanted to do and began to make preparations. He took his jacket off and laid it onto the cold stone floor of the changing room.

'Lie down on your back,' he said to Tom. The lad complied and stretched himself out with his underwear now pulled back on. Charlie stared in silence as James unbuttoned his trousers

162

and pulled out his cock. It was as stiff as a board and trickling a clear fluid of excitement from the tip. He knelt between Tom's legs and yanked down his underpants. He gestured for the lad to raise his legs into the air and then spat onto the end of his fingers. With a roughness only comparable to that which Tom had used on him when he was initiated in the barn, James jabbed the saliva-drenched fingers up inside his anal passage. The boy let out a hiss of discomfort and his stomach muscles clenched together. He revolved the digits inside the lad until he was as lubricated as possible.

With Tom's legs held up in the air, James guided his prick towards the opening and began to work it inside. The lad flinched a little as the thing slid into him, but he was a hefty young man and it was obvious that he would be able to take the pain. James, however, knew no mercy and plunged the full length of his penis into the lad, right up to the hilt. After a few seconds James started to notice that the muscles that had clenched so tightly around his member were now beginning to loosen and accept the stiff invader. Tom's face showed the difference. The pained expression subsided into one of acceptance and there was even a hint of enjoyment about his face.

James moved his cock in and out of the boy, and with every thrust a shudder of pleasure engulfed his body. All the while he was sucking Tom, he had imagined what it would be like to actually penetrate him. Now, with his cock deep inside the lad's tight passage, James felt elated and empowered.

He noticed that Tom's member was once again standing up stiff; proof enough that the anal stimulation he provided was working wonders. Not only was the lad hard as a board, but there was also to be seen a steady flow of sticky juice oozing from the tip of his cock and onto his tensed stomach. James dabbed a finger into the liquid and tasted it. It was exactly like that which he had just tasted, only before he had the added joy of taking the stuff directly from its source.

James had become so engrossed in probing the lad's arse that

163

he had completely forgotten about Charlie. The young lad stood watching the boys in amazement, a huge erection poking out of his underwear. James knew that there was plenty of room for him to join in with the fun and he made a gesture towards him. Charlie's eyes lit up as if this was the moment he had been waiting for. James made another movement to suggest that the lad pull off his underwear and come closer.

'I'm sure Tom will help you out with that,' he said, pointing towards the lad's quivering penis. 'Turn around.'

For a moment it looked as if he did not understand the instructions, but after a little careful thought he seemed to have worked out where he was meant to go. He knelt over Tom's face, with his back to James and his arse in the air. He slowly lowered himself down onto all fours and angled his straining erection towards Tom's mouth. Tom seemed so excited by his anal treatment that he was prepared to add to anyone else's enjoyment, and with great gusto he gulped down Charlie's cock.

It was a pleasure, while James penetrated the lad, to see the other boy being sucked off. Because of the extreme angle he had to put himself in to reach Tom's mouth, Charlie had his arse pushed up into the air, and from where he was kneeling, James had a perfect view of the lad's exposed crack and arsehole.

He could not resist leaning forward a little and gently kissing the boy's bottom. Charlie gave a moan of pleasure as if to encourage further attention and James began to tongue the soft, pink ring. This made him even more excited and desperate to relieve himself, and he thrust his cock deeper into Tom, whose moans of pleasure were now almost inaudible. The lad's mouth was full of Charlie's prick, and James could see him desperately sucking as if this was what he had always wanted to do but never had the courage to ask.

The hole now felt wet and warm around his penis; the friction from his relentless lunges adding to the enjoyment. James could feel the semen building up at the very base of

himself and he longed for release. He continued to delve into Charlie's tight arsehole with both fingers and tongue, opening the boy up as much as possible and driving himself deep inside. The smell and taste of his boyish hole made James wild with desire and he pumped Tom even harder.

All of a sudden Charlie started to pant loudly and push his hips aggressively towards Tom's mouth. James was amazed at how quickly the lad was brought to a climax. He watched as he shuddered and gasped for air and as Tom lapped away at his shooting prick. The sight was enough to send James to the brink and he felt the overwhelming sensation of his own semen pushing itself upwards and through the swollen tip. He lunged forward and drove his cock viciously into Tom's arse and let a torrent of pent-up seed spill out. The release was magnificent and James felt that he would not be able to stop spending. The tightness of the lad's arsehole and his continual gasps of shock and pleasure made it even more enjoyable to shoot his load up into him. He could feel the final drops of come seeping from the head of his penis and he fell against Charlie's arse as though it were a pillow.

All three boys collapsed in an exhausted pile, spent and drained. James looked over at Barnaby who was also on his knees in front of Tank. They had finished their games and looked as exhausted as everyone else.

'Trust you to be greedy,' said Barnaby with a chuckle. 'Wasn't one enough for you?'

James smiled at him, too tired to speak.

The two cousins sat on a bench and watched the boys get into their kits. Memories of school and watching the other lads get ready for games came flooding back to James. If he could have known then what would happen to him only a few years down the line then perhaps he'd not have minded so much the frustration of never being able to do anything at school but look.

The village lads slowly dressed themselves in the familiar garb of the football player: jockstrap, long socks, tight blue shorts, gold coloured top and black boots. As Tank bent over to do up his laces, James could not help staring at the lines that the canvas straps of his jockstrap made across his full, rounded arse. The lad looked so lovely and innocent, as if there was nothing suggestive about what he was wearing or how he held himself.

When the boys had nearly finished dressing the handle of the door rattled and there was a sharp knock.

'James, can you unlock the door?' asked Barnaby. James got up and did so. No sooner had he turned the key than the rest of the team came rushing in, chattering and messing around like a bunch of schoolboys, and, in effect, that's all that they were. Most of them looked no more than eighteen or nineteen. James glanced around and counted the heads.

'There are only ten boys here,' he said to anyone who cared to listen. 'Where's Gabriel?' He had suddenly realised who was missing and felt agitated and annoyed. There were only twenty minutes to go before the match began and there was no sign of Gabriel.

'I don't know,' said Tom. 'He didn't say anything to us about being late.'

'We're counting on him,' added one of the team. 'He's our best attack player.'

James and Barnaby sat with the rest of the family and waited for the match to begin. They were positioned directly in line with the kick-off point and thus had the best view of the action to come. James was worried about Gabriel. He could not imagine why he was not here. The day before when they had met for their picnic he had sounded so enthusiastic, as if it would be the event of the year, not to be missed on any account.

'He'll be here,' Barnaby whispered into his ear. 'I'm sure of it.' James hoped that his cousin was right. However, it was

already after the starting time and both teams were huddled together exchanging last minute words and the referee had positioned himself in the centre of the pitch. He blew the whistle and the team captains from Rolvenden and Fryhurst came towards him. The game was about to begin.

All of a sudden there came a shout from the other side of the field and everyone looked across to see who it was. James's face lit up as Gabriel came running over the pitch and towards the changing room.

'Give me two minutes and I'll be with you,' he shouted.

He soon came back out again in his kit and the game began. All the boys were enthusiastic and desperate for their team to win. Within the first ten minutes two goals were scored, one by Rolvenden and one by Fryhurst. Gabriel excelled himself, tackling the opposition's finest players and scoring a second goal for Rolvenden. James cheered so loudly that Barnaby had to tell him not to shout so much. It was a pleasure just to watch the bright, athletic young men racing around the pitch, putting their skills to the test. They certainly were Rolvenden's finest and James became totally engrossed in the action.

By half-time the score was two all and the pressure was certainly on. Fryhurst had won for the past two years, Barnaby told him, and this time the village was determined to take back the title. Gabriel came over during the break and James congratulated him on his magnificent goal. The lad looked lovely in his kit – now dirty with dust and earth from the pitch – which seemed to highlight every aspect of the fitness of his body. James could not stop himself from staring down at the boy's crotch while they talked, and later watching the swagger of his tight buttocks as he walked back over to join the rest of his team.

The second half had hardly even started when Gabriel fell to the ground after attempting to tackle one of the boys. James stood up to see what had happened. The referee was telling him to relax and trying to rub his leg, but every time he

touched it Gabriel let out a yelp in pain. He heard someone say that he should rest and the substitute could take his place. James moved towards the centre of the pitch.

'Where are you going?' Barnaby called out.

'To see if he's all right,' replied James, and he crossed to where the lad was lying. 'Gabriel, are you badly hurt?'

'Yes, sir, I think so,' he said.

'Let's see if you can stand up.' James bent over and put an arm around his shoulder and helped him to his feet. 'Do you think you're able to walk on it?'

Gabriel limped around for a moment. 'I can walk on it but I don't think I'll be able to play football on it.' The boy looked sad and James did not know what to say to make him feel better. The referee suggested that he be taken back to the changing room to rest. James volunteered to look after him and the two boys slowly made their way back to the little brick building.

Once inside James sat his friend down on one of the benches and gently removed his shoes and socks. 'Is that a bit better?'

'Yes, but my leg's still very sore,' said Gabriel. 'And I'm so disappointed at having to drop out of the match. It was just getting good.'

James felt very sorry for the boy. He knew how much he'd been looking forward to playing and now it was all spoilt. Gabriel sat on the bench clutching his leg, a sad expression on his face. James could think of nothing to say that would make the boy feel better so they talked of other things. 'I didn't think you were ever going to get here. Everyone was really worried.'

'Oh, well, that wasn't really my fault.'

'So, what happened?' James asked.

'It was my girl. We had a bit of a row and I couldn't get away until we'd had it out good and proper. Then I looked at my watch and it was nearly midday.'

'What was the upshot of the argument?'

'I decided to stop seeing her.' James felt a little ray of hope

light up inside him. 'I thought it'd be for the best and all.' James remained silent. 'Would you give my leg a rub?'

'Of course.' James was only too pleased to be asked to touch the lad in any possible way. Gabriel moved himself until he was lying down on the bench with his leg up. James softly massaged the lad's leg. He could feel how tense the muscles were and gently tried to relax them by rubbing along their edges with his thumbs. Gabriel let out a low moan and closed his eyes.

Just the feel of the lad's firm leg, covered with soft hairs, made James's cock swell up in his trousers. Even though Gabriel was injured and he should be concentrating on making him comfortable, he could not stop thinking how beautiful he was and how much he would love to kiss the boy's pouting red lips. He ran his hands all along the length of the leg, from the ankle right to the top of his thigh where his shorts ended.

It was either the movement of his fingers or that strange sexual tension that always plagues one's loins after physical exertion that began to produce a hardening in Gabriel's shorts. Whatever the reason, James could not avoid the fact that his friend was becoming terribly stiff. Every time his hands worked their way to the very top of his leg he could see the lad's cock twitch through the tight material of his shorts. It was too obvious to ignore – Gabriel was very excited.

James was overtaken with desire and his hands gradually made their way up the inside of Gabriel's shorts. Gabriel did not move away but seemed to want the hands to travel even further. He parted his legs a fraction to allow easier access, and James pushed his fingers into the gap between the boy's thigh and balls. He could feel the soft cotton of his jockstrap and the outline of his cock.

All of a sudden Gabriel sat up and kissed James full on the mouth. Their lips parted and tongues slid from one mouth into the other. It was the most lovely feeling James could think of. He had never been properly kissed by another boy, apart from once by Sam in the summer house, and now he knew that he

would never want anyone else to do it but Gabriel. His mouth tasted exactly how James imagined it would – warm and slippery and boyish.

They remained pressed together in embrace for some minutes, James not wanting to let go of the boy in case this time, as before, he would run out of the room in horror. However, when at last they did move apart, Gabriel did not back away or make his excuses. Instead he smiled sweetly and pushed James's face down to his crotch. It was obvious that the lad was desperate to be sucked and he wanted James to be the one to do it.

He kissed Gabriel's crotch through the material and then, with the lad's help, he pulled the shorts off. He sniffed at the jockstrap which was drenched in sweat. There was a sticky patch of clear fluid seeping through the canvas where the tip of his cock rested. James put his tongue to it and tasted the salty pre-come. It was obvious that Gabriel could not wait any longer to feel lips around his prick and he pulled his jockstrap down at the front and out leapt his magnificent erection. James took hold of it, but did not immediately put it in his mouth. He wrapped his hand around the thick shaft and drew back the foreskin. The head looked swollen and sensitive. He extended his tongue and teased the tip, in the process ingesting the droplet of cream at the end.

Gabriel exhaled a deep sigh and the knob seemed to expand. With his hand still tight around the organ, James moved his tongue down towards the lad's sweat-drenched balls. They were constricted within their heavy sack and he began to lick at them, amazed by how interesting they tasted, flavoured with a mixture of perspiration and natural bodily musk. James let his tongue roam around them, occasionally taking a ball into his mouth and gently sucking on it. Gabriel wriggled and panted, which only made him more eager to tease the lad.

He lifted the balls and licked the smooth surface underneath them, inhaling the aroma of the boy's perineum. It was as if

every movement of his mouth was an attempt to both relieve the pain of the boy's injury and at the same time to arouse his sexual yearning. James was, in a sense, the helpless victim of his own lust, unable to stop himself from exploring every hidden recess and healing it with his mouth.

After he had tasted those lovely secret places, he could not stop himself from returning to the surface and swallowing Gabriel's straining cock. With a firm grip on the boy's glands he took the head of his prick between his lips and ran his tongue around the distended knob. A hand at the back of his head forced him to take down the whole length, and soon he was sucking away more deeply than he had ever done before.

James was simultaneously at the lad's mercy, and yet master of his pleasure. Every movement of his mouth controlled the way Gabriel reacted. Saliva dribbled down his chin and onto the lad's balls. He had never felt so at one with another human being as he did now with his love in him.

'Oh, James,' the boy cried out breathlessly, 'I don't think I can hold myself back any longer.' Immediately he pulled his mouth away and let the boy's cock slap back against his football top. 'Why did you stop?'

'I don't want you to spend so soon,' James panted. 'I must have more of you before then.' Gabriel looked confused. 'Turn over onto your front.' Gabriel did as he was instructed and laid himself prostrate on the bench. James's prick twitched violently at the sight before him. Even though he still had the jockstrap on, because of the very nature of the supportive garment, the lad's arse cheeks were totally exposed. The waistband and straps framed his buttocks and pointed downwards towards James's ultimate goal – his tight hole.

With great care, not wanting to make the lad's injury even worse, James parted his legs so that they hung down either side of the bench. Then he started to caress the firm, heavy cheeks and slowly parted them to reveal the long strip of muscular flesh between. James put his face close to the area in question and

James pulled his fingers out and took in a deep breath. He could still taste the boy, as if his arse was still in his face. He lingered over him, admiring the shape and fullness of his buttocks and how pleasing they looked in the jockstrap.

Gabriel stood up and looked James in the eye. He then took off his football shirt and approached him. Before James knew what was happening he had been grabbed and kissed – the most passionate kiss – and he could feel the boy's strong hands all over his body tugging and undoing his clothes. This was more than he could ever have hoped for. There was a look about him that told James that this was more than simply boyish lust. All the while he was being undressed, Gabriel was kissing his lips, face and neck. James trembled in the youth's muscular arms. He felt completely at his mercy, there was nothing he wouldn't let him do. His body was there for Gabriel's pleasure.

'You don't know how long I've wanted to do this with you, sir,' Gabriel whispered into his ear. James's trousers and shirt fell to the floor and he felt the lad's hands pulling at his underwear. Soon he was completely naked and trembling in the boy's protective arms. 'It's so hard to tell you, sir, you being a gentleman and all.'

'I've been thinking the same thing, you fool!' said James. 'I never thought you'd ever really care for me.'

'Oh, I do, sir. I do.' Gabriel's hands were everywhere. James could feel them all over his arse and between his legs. The boy could not seem to get enough of him. James could not stop himself from gasping when he felt the country lad's rough hands rubbing away at his cock and balls. He felt like he might explode at any moment.

'Sir, there's something I'd like to do to you,' said Gabriel. 'If you'd let me.'

'What is it?' James was suffused with pleasure. 'Anything!' The boy could do no wrong in his eyes.

'I'd like to kiss you just the same as you kissed me.' And without waiting for an answer he turned James around and

bent him over the bench. Immediately he started kissing him all over his bottom, working his way towards the area between the cheeks. He could feel Gabriel's tongue hovering near to his most sensitive area. Then, all of a sudden, the lad parted his buttocks fully and pushed his tongue into the arsehole. It felt like he might pass out at any moment. James had to turn around and make sure he wasn't dreaming. As he looked back he saw Gabriel's face buried between his buttocks and felt the accute sensation of the lad's slippery tongue working away on his tight little hole.

The boy seemed utterly engrossed in his arse and not only used his tongue but also his fingers, opening James up and sliding the spittle-covered digits deep inside him. All this only added to his sexual frustration and he longed to be relieved. Also, the feeling of the lad's fingers inside him made him dream of something larger filling him and thrusting itself about in him.

'Sir?' said Gabriel. 'Could we lie down together?' James wasn't sure what the boy meant. 'Like a man and a woman would.' He felt arms once again around him and before he knew they were on the floor together writhing around, kissing and running their hands over one another's bodies. The ground was cold, but this did not bother James. Just being with his love was enough to make all other distractions vanish.

James was suddenly on his back and Gabriel was on top of him, rubbing his hands over his chest and down to his cock. He knew exactly what the lad wanted to do, and it was fine by him. He opened his legs and raised them slightly off the ground and immediately felt the lad's stiff prick between his thighs. Gabriel pushed himself backwards and forwards, rubbing his member all the while against James's legs and buttocks.

James stopped him. 'Why don't you put it inside me?'

'I wouldn't want to hurt you, sir,' said Gabriel.

'No, you wouldn't hurt me.' He kissed him tenderly on the lips and smiled. 'I'd love you to.' Without giving a reply the lad simply spat on his finger and wiped the saliva over the head

and shaft of his violently erect cock. 'Put some inside me as well. It'll make it go in easier.' Gabriel spat on his fingers once again, but this time he guided them carefully towards James's arsehole. They felt cold and wet as they slid inside, but James knew that what would follow them would be much warmer. His bottom slowly relaxed around the lad's digits.

Gabriel then grasped his own penis by the base and angled it down towards its ultimate goal. James raised his legs into the air as far as they would comfortably go and waited for the boy to move himself inside. He maintained eye contact all the time while pushing his prick inside, and James felt the bodily connection between the two of them. The tip of the swollen member touched the ring and made him tingle. Then Gabriel, with a look of total concentration on his face, jabbed his cock further inside and he felt himself opening up, being penetrated.

At first the lad's penis felt so huge that James thought it would never be able to get all the way in, but he was wrong. He put his hands on the boy's manly buttocks and guided him carefully inside. He was so gentle and so beautiful that James could do nothing but open up and allow him entry.

'Is that all right, sir?' Gabriel asked. 'I'm not hurting you, am I?'

'No. It feels nice.' With his hands clasping onto the boy's arse cheeks James could feel the full length inside him and he breathed a wonderful sigh of relief. 'Are you right inside me?' he asked.

'Yes. I think so.' But just to make sure, James put his hand down to the lad's crotch and held onto his balls. It was true, the thick cock was fully inside him, right up to the hilt. James squeezed his balls and then returned his hands to the rounded and tensed buttocks as they began to drive, with all their force, Gabriel's prick in and out of him. The feeling was magnificent and sent shudders through James's body. Every movement made him more accustomed to the sensation and soon his bottom was welcoming the stiff organ as if it had always been there.

His own penis was as erect as it had ever been and was leaking a steady stream of fluid over his stomach. James could not resist wrapping a hand around the base and gliding the foreskin back and forth over the slippery knob. The feeling was overpowering and his head was filled with the image of the boy he loved thrusting his prick deep inside him.

James could see the expression of concentration and ecstasy on Gabriel's face as he pounded away at his arse. The lad looked as if he were about to explode and James too could tell that he was nearing his own climax. Gabriel began to pant aggressively and then all of a sudden let out a cry that signalled only one thing – the fact that he was spilling his seed. At the same moment, and triggered by Gabriel's violent thrust, James shot a jet of semen over his stomach. More spurts followed, driven out by the lad's persistent pounding.

The two boys spent at the same time, and afterwards collapsed into one another's arms. James felt exhausted, his chest and stomach covered with his own spunk, and Gabriel's discharge still inside him. The lad's penis slowly slipped out from his anus and a feeling of calm relief flooded through him.

'I'd never expected it to be so good,' said Gabriel. 'It's lovely and warm inside you.'

James smiled at his lover and kissed him on the lips. 'Thank you,' he whispered.

The boys showered themselves and dressed. The game was over. They could hear cheers and applause coming from the field outside and they opened the door and joined the players and supporters. James helped Gabriel over to one of the seats, near to the Compton-Crofts, and sat down next to him.

'Feeling better now, Gabriel?' Barnaby asked.

'Yes, thank you, sir.'

'I bet you are!' His cousin always seemed to know a little too much, and James threw him a look of mild annoyance.

'Who won?' asked Gabriel.

'We did.'

The lad looked thrilled. Even though he'd had to pull out of the match, Rolvenden had still taken the title back.

'I think we'd better take you home,' said James. 'You're still in a poor state.' Gabriel nodded his head. 'Come back to Sunningdale. You can rest there. Do you think that'll be all right with your mother, Barnaby?'

'Oh, I'm sure.'

James helped his friend back to the house and up to his bedroom. There he gently undressed the lad, still in his football kit, and put him into his own bed. He tucked him up and sat down in a chair. Gabriel looked calm and at peace with the world. He gave a warm smile and closed his eyes.

James felt overjoyed to not only have his lover in his bed, but also to know that perhaps they might be together at last. His holiday was certainly working out well. There was nothing that made him want to go home. London seemed like a horrible recurring dream from his childhood – a dream that he didn't have any more. Rolvenden was the only place that he wanted to spend his time.

After dinner James came back upstairs early, having made his excuses to his aunt and cousins, and quietly opened the bedroom door. Gabriel was lying in his bed wide awake and staring out of the window. The boys smiled at one another.

'Why don't you come to bed, sir?' James couldn't care less whether someone came in or not. He was with the boy he loved and he wanted to lie down with him. He had never spent the night with another man and now was the time to do it. He took off his clothes and slipped in beside the lad. The bed was narrow, but as they embraced one another, it didn't seem so bad. Just being beside one another was enough to give them instant erections.

Gabriel reached down in the bed and slipped his hand down the front of James's underwear. It felt so nice and warm lying there together and James was in heaven with the lad's fingers

playing with his stiff penis. He returned the gesture and soon their underpants had been discarded and they lay naked next to one another. Their lips met and they exchanged a deep, wet kiss.

James watched as his friend disappeared below the covers and he felt his lips encircling his cock and the smooth sensation of the lad's tongue wrapping itself around the swollen head. He let out a little sigh, knowing that it would not take long for Gabriel to once again make him spend.

Nine

James opened his eyes and began to gain consciousness. He remembered the most wonderful dream that he'd been having about Gabriel being in bed with him and the two of them making love together. It felt a little cramped in the bed and when he turned around James could barely believe his eyes. 'It wasn't a dream,' he said out loud.

'What?' Gabriel muttered, still half-asleep.

'Nothing,' he whispered. The events of the previous day came flooding back to him: the football match, the changing room and settling down for the night with the boy he loved. James reached out and ran his fingers through the lad's soft locks. He made a low noise of pleasure and slowly opened his eyes, blinking at the light that crept in through the edges of the shutters.

'How are you this morning?' James asked.

'Fine.'

'How's your leg feeling?'

'A lot better, I think,' Gabriel replied.

James could not resist leaning over in the bed and kissing the boy on the lips. As usual first thing in the morning he felt excited, and his prick was as hard as a board. This morning,

however, he had someone next to him who might be able to offer some assistance. Gabriel parted his lips and their tongues touched inside the other's warm mouth. James put his arms around him and they embraced. His hands ran down the lad's back and rested on his firm arse cheeks. They felt warm and muscular. He let the tips of his fingers explore the sweaty crack and they came to rest on Gabriel's tight arsehole. He knew that the hole had never been probed with anything other than his tongue and fingers and James hoped that perhaps the lad would soon let him go further.

He could feel hands rubbing his cock and exploring between his legs. He loved having the fleshy strip between his balls and arsehole gently touched. It made his cock spring about with excitement. James responded in a similar way and began to stretch back and forth the lad's pliable foreskin. He too was hard and there was a slippery fluid escaping from the tip of his long member. He slipped under the bed covers and kissed Gabriel's chest. His body was warm and firm, and he lingered over the pert nipples, which he gently clasped his teeth around and suckled on, as if he were a baby drinking from his mother's breast. The lad gave a boyish groan and James moved his mouth downwards.

As he started kissing Gabriel's stomach he felt hands on the back of his head pushing him down onto the straining erection which jutted up towards his face. James took the hint and moved his mouth so that it was level with the lad's prick. He could see how excited the boy was from the amount of pre-come that had trickled out of his cock and down the side of the swollen knob. James inhaled the sweet smell of his genitals and then took the tip into his mouth and started to suck. The flavour of the sticky secretion was so fresh and lovely that James's own prick trembled and he yearned to relieve himself.

Before long the whole length of Gabriel's prick was deep inside his mouth and he used his lips and tongue to stimulate the stiff pole. With one hand at the base, gently wanking the

shaft, and the other gripped around the lad's heavy sack, James eased the cock in and out of his mouth.

He was totally under the covers while he worked on Gabriel's erection, and the lad's hands held onto his face, as if he wanted to feel his shaft sliding about in James's mouth. The smell that filled his nostrils was so intense that it was as if he had become one with the lad's body. His mouth moved in frantic jerks up and down the stiff organ and he squeezed the balls as hard as he could without hurting the youth.

Boys being as they are, easy to excite and make spend in the morning, James soon heard the breathless panting and moans coming from Gabriel, which could only mean one thing – it would not be long before he spilled his semen. He frantically sucked and wanked the swollen penis until he heard the moans stop and the lad hold his breath. At the same time the head became rock hard and a violent jet of spunk shot into James's mouth and he eagerly swallowed down the salty fluid. This was followed by six or seven shorter bursts and soon his mouth was filled with his lover's semen. James gulped down as much as he could, but there was such an amount that some trickled over his lips and ran down his chin.

Gabriel's body was still trembling even after he had finished spurting, and James placed a hand on his stomach to feel the final spasms as his balls pumped out the last of the salty liquid. He drunk down everything, licked his lips and cleaned up the head of the lad's trembling penis. Gabriel exhaled a sigh of relief and tiredness. James, however, was not so relieved and his cock ached for some attention.

'Gabriel,' he said, returning to the same level as the boy, 'there's something I'd really like to do to you, if you'd let me.'

'What's that?' He was still out of breath from his exhausting climax and spoke slowly and quietly.

'Could I make love to you, like you did to me yesterday?'

'Of course,' he replied. 'But you must be gentle. I've never had it done to me before, so it might be a little tight.'

'I'll be careful.' James pulled the covers off the two of them and once again slipped down in the bed. 'Turn over.' Gabriel stretched himself out with his chin resting on his arms and his bottom exposed. 'Can you pass me a pillow?' said James.

'What for?'

'You'll see.' James took the pillow that was handed to him. 'Raise your hips a bit.' He slipped it under the boy whose bottom was now raised into the air. 'Makes it easier for me to do it, and more comfortable for you.' James went to work. He parted Gabriel's legs as much as he could and massaged his buttocks. He could just about see the lad's face from where he was positioned and it had a sleepy, content expression.

James prised the cheeks apart and gazed at the pretty little opening. It looked so small and tight that he wondered whether he'd ever be able to get his cock up there. Without delaying any longer he placed the tip of his tongue to the puckered hole and immediately started to moisten it with his saliva. He knew that if he relaxed the lad and opened him up beforehand, then when it came to actually penetrating him it would make things a lot easier.

He ran his tongue up and down the lad's hairy groove and dipped it back inside the tiny hole, which was gradually becoming more relaxed. Gabriel writhed about, rubbing himself over the sheets and making boyish noises, as James applied the full force of his tongue. With his hands rubbing the rounded arse cheeks, he delved deeply inside. The lad seemed to open up easily. He was obviously built for the act.

'I'm afraid I haven't got any Vaseline,' said James.

'That's all right, sir.' Gabriel glanced over his shoulder and smiled. 'Just use spit.' James spat into the palm of his hand and rubbed the liquid over the head of his aching cock and down the length of the erect shaft. It felt lovely stroking his prick like that and James knew that if he continued for much longer it would make him spurt.

He used the rest of the saliva on Gabriel's arsehole, letting

two of his fingers slide inside the lad and travel deeply down his anal passage. He let out a little gasp, but James continued to lubricate him and soon had deposited all the spittle inside him and was rubbing the last drops around the rim of his hole.

'Are you ready?' he asked. Gabriel made a little noise which he took to be a 'yes' and he angled his cock down towards the lad's arsehole. Using just one hand James parted the two globes and moved his prick between them. For the first time the tip came into contact with the lad's soft opening and he heard Gabriel give out a sigh as the head of his cock glided inside. The hole dilated and allowed the swollen knob to enter its inner recesses. It felt so thrilling, with the tightly muscled hole clamped around his cock, but James knew that this was the easy part. He now had to insert the rest of the shaft, without hurting the lad too badly.

His need for fulfilment drove James on and he slowly pushed the rest of his penis inside. He could feel the muscles gradually accepting his intrusion and a stifled groan came drifting from the direction of Gabriel's mouth. It seemed to go in easier than he had imagined. The lad's arse, even though it had never been touched, seemed to naturally take to his cock, as if one had been built to fit the other.

James put his full weight onto his knees and elbows and used them to lever his prick in and out of the boy's arsehole. The tightness and warmth of the hole made him quiver with excitement and James pushed himself deeply inside, moving his penis about in the comfort of the lad's bottom. To think that he could possess such a strong youth with nothing but his cock, and put him at the mercy of his passion, shocked and excited him.

James thrust himself hard into the lad, whose face twisted into an expression of discomfort. Seeing Gabriel writhe around made him even more excited and he pushed his cock in and out as hard as he could. The lad's arse felt hot and slippery and he knew that it would not take very much to make him spend.

The feeling of being right up inside his love was sublime and his balls ached for release.

Gabriel moved his arse in rhythm with his thrusts, as if he were echoing them in a pleasured response. The little whimpering sounds that escaped his lips made James yearn to spill his seed inside the lad and he pushed his cock in deep, at the same time rubbing his hands over the muscular buttocks. He could feel the blood pumping through Gabriel, and the flinching movements the boy made as he slid in and out thrilled him to the core.

James realised that he could not hold himself back any longer, the drawing of the lad's tight passage on his cock was too much, and he let out a long spurt of semen into his arse. He could feel each explosion of spunk begin in his balls and work its way along the shaft and out of the tip with such impact that he felt certain Gabriel would be able to feel it hitting him inside. As he spent James gripped hold of the boy's arse cheeks and forced his prick right inside his tight hole. He could feel the final bursts of semen and he fell against Gabriel's back, panting and exhausted.

'Are you all right?' he asked.

'Fine, sir,' Gabriel replied. He too looked out of breath and drained. James softly stroked his shoulders and ran the tips of his fingers through the thick hair at the back of his head. His cock was still inside the lad, and the sheer force of being in there meant he was able to stay hard whether he wanted to or not.

'Did it feel nice?' James asked.

'Oh, yes, sir, it felt lovely. So big and hard inside me,' said Gabriel, turning his head and smiling at him. 'I thought it would be painful, and it was a little at first. But as soon as you'd been in me for a minute or so, it started to feel much nicer.'

With the utmost care James pulled his cock out and breathed a lovely sigh of relief. The two boys sank into one another's arms and closed their eyes.

★ ★ ★

James and Gabriel kissed once more and got out of the bed. They'd already missed breakfast and the best part of the day. As the boys were dressing themselves there came a knock at the door.

'Who is it?' James called out.

'It's Barnaby,' came the voice, and before waiting for a command to enter he flung open the door. 'Ah, there you are.' He slumped into a chair and crossed his legs. 'You missed breakfast. Mother was terribly curious. I had to make up all sorts of terrible excuses.'

'I'm sorry. I hope she wasn't too suspicious.' James looked a little worried.

'Oh, no, for goodness' sake, she couldn't care less.' Barnaby lounged back in the seat. 'I'm sure she's seen everything. And with *my* behaviour she'll be used to it.' James looked relieved. 'Now, what have you two been up to?' Both boys blushed and looked at one another shyly.

'Barnaby! Do you have to be so . . .' James tried to find the word, 'forward? You've embarrassed Gabriel.'

'Embarrassed *you* more like.' All three of them laughed and James put his arm around Gabriel's waist. 'I've got a proposition to make to you.' The boys looked confused. 'Now Gabriel's joined us, I thought we ought to have a celebration with the other boys.'

'What do you mean?' James asked.

'What I mean is I've sent a note to Tom and Tank to invite them to meet us down by the river at dusk. I've told them that they can bring anyone else they like and we'll bring the drink. What do you say?'

'Sounds like a good idea to me,' said James. He turned to his friend. 'Will you come?' Gabriel looked blissfully enthusiastic and nodded as he laced up his boots.

James had arranged to meet Barnaby down by the river, because he wanted to spend the day with Gabriel, and that's exactly

what they did. Most of it was spent getting in and out of bed, and James was happy just to be with the lad.

They walked side by side down to the old barn and Gabriel confessed that he was terribly excited. He told James how he'd longed to get involved with the boys' games, but had not dared to for fear that someone might have found out. James had liberated him and now he felt comfortable with the idea, and elated that today he would be given the opportunity.

Barnaby was waiting with Tom, Tank and Sam down by the river. The sky was darkening and the warmth of the day was fading into a cool night. The two boys approached the others and welcoming greetings were exchanged.

'How are you, Gabe?' said Tom.

'I'm fine,' he replied.

'So, you want to join in at last, do you?' Gabriel looked a little embarrassed and smirked nervously. 'I'll take that as a yes then, shall I? Of course you're the only one here who isn't in the gang.'

Everyone passed into the old barn, with the exception of Barnaby and Sam, who said they would rather be alone for a moment. Tom always took charge of the initiation, being the oldest and most established member, and he marched Gabriel to the centre of the room and stood him there. James thought that the lad looked a bit worried, so he approached him and whispered in his ear that everything would be fine.

Tom walked up to the lad and tied a thick strip of black material over his eyes and made him drop down onto his knees. 'Right, don't speak, just do as you're told.' Gabriel looked so helpless kneeling there. James knew exactly what would happen next and he feared for his friend. 'You go first,' said Tom. 'After all he's your special friend.'

James felt a little nervous at the thought of having to thrust his cock into the boy's mouth so brutally, but it was all part of the initiation and it had to be done. Tom put a hand on his shoulder and guided James towards the place where he must

186

stand. He felt the rough boy's hands rubbing his crotch from behind. He already had a stiff cock, and Tom's touch made him feel even more eager to get his release. His trousers and underwear were undone for him and his cock sprang out. Tom took complete control of the operation. 'Now, Gabe, open you mouth and swallow this.' The lad did as he was told and opened his mouth wide while Tom angled James's cock inside.

Gabriel immediately started to suck on him furiously, like he had never seen him suck before. James pushed his prick deeply into the lad's mouth, using the full force of his hips to drive the thing right down his throat. It felt odd with the other boys watching him, but there was a strange thrill to be derived from being an exhibitionist.

All the while James was pushing into the lad's mouth, he could feel Tom's hands taking down his underpants at the back and stroking his arse. The lad's fingers were creeping towards the crack between his cheeks which only added to his feeling of pleasure. Gabriel's mouth was wet and slippery and his cock slid in and out easily. The lad reached forward and grasped hold of James's balls. At the same time Tom's fingers entered his arsehole.

The overall feeling was sublime, every sensitive part of him was being stimulated and he knew that he could do nothing but spend. It was lovely to be able to relieve himself in his lover's mouth and a squirt of semen shot out from the tip of his cock and into Gabriel. The lad was obviously enjoying himself for he gulped away and James could see him swallowing the sperm down and eagerly sucking for more. He gave the lad a mouthful and when he was finished pulled his cock out and stood still, the final drops of fluid dripping from the head. Gabriel moved his face forward as if to try to take another taste of James's cock, but Tom had already guided James away. That was the end of his turn.

'Tank,' he said. 'You next.' The lad nodded and approached the kneeling boy.

James stepped back. He was out of breath and exhausted. It had felt so good to have his prick in the young man's mouth, and there was something terribly exciting about him not being able to see, but to just be made to relieve one boy after another. James watched as Tom moved the next lad into position. Tank's cock looked long and threatening. He wondered whether Gabriel, having had hardly any experience of such things, would be able to accommodate it in his soft little mouth. His fears were quelled, however, and the lad opened his mouth wide and the stiff organ slid right inside.

Even though he felt an exclusive right over the lad, James did not mind him doing things with other boys. This was an ancient custom of the countryside, something James felt must always have happened and always would. The boys were simply exercising their power to be young, carefree and sexually excitable. He knew that Gabriel had been desperate to join in and now he had found the courage to do so. There was also something terribly thrilling about watching the boy he adored frantically sucking at another lad's prick.

Tom stood directly behind Tank and fondled his bottom as he had James's. The lad looked pleased to be able to push his cock inside the moist cavity. He grunted and moaned as Gabriel let his lips caress the hard shaft and James waited in eager anticipation for the moment when he would begin to ejaculate.

He did not have to wait long, for almost at once he heard the familiar sound of the lad coming to his climax. He knew that he was spurting because Gabriel's face looked desperate and excited, and he gulped at the lad's prick as if it were delivering the very milk of life. Tank's balls were tightly pressed against the base of his cock and he was holding onto the sides of Gabriel's face in order to push as much of himself into his mouth as was possible. James imagined how wonderful it must taste and he felt a slight pang of jealousy towards Gabriel who was experiencing all these things for the first time.

Tank pulled his cock out of the lad's mouth and let out a long sigh. Gabriel looked exhausted. James thought how his mouth must ache after the two stiff organs he had been forced to take.

'You boys,' Tom ordered, 'help him onto the table.' They helped Gabriel to his feet and guided him towards the table. Tom indicated that he should be undressed and laid down on his back. The boys took off his shirt and breeches and moved him onto the hard wooden table, at the same time checking that the blindfold was still tightly in place. Tom positioned himself between the lad's parted legs and the other two stood at either side of him. They bound Gabriel's hands to the table legs so that he was unable to move the upper part of his body.

Tom yanked down his underpants and threw them onto the floor. He now had unrestricted access to the area between the lad's thighs. James watched as he pushed his legs apart, spat on his fingers and drove them deeply into Gabriel's arse. There was a pained look on his face as the digits worked their way into and around his arsehole. James could not resist stroking his lover's chest, which lay fully exposed on the table before him. He gently squeezed his nipples and caressed his smooth stomach.

Tom took his fingers out and placed them with the tip of his hard cock, which he had whipped out from his trousers and angled between the lad's thighs. He held Gabriel's legs in the air in order to open up his secret orifice and fill it with his frightening shaft. James felt for the lad as he watched the swollen head of Tom's prick cut into him. This was followed closely by the rest of the length, which he violently rammed inside.

Gabriel let out a pained whimper and dug his fingers into the legs of the table. James could see Tom's cock pounding away at the lad's arse, being pushed right the way up, and then dragged back out until it looked as if the stiff member would slip completely free. However, after every retraction there

came another thrust forwards and the penis was pumped back inside.

James could hear both the lads panting. Tom took short, aggressive gulps of air, sounding as if he were desperately fighting against his own release, and Gabriel made groaning noises at the back of his throat, as though suppressing the urge to cry out in pain. James continued to let his hands travel across the lad's muscular chest and they eventually came to rest on his cock and balls. The stiff pole felt warm in his hand and he started to jerk the foreskin backwards and forwards. He imagined what it must feel like to have Tom's huge length up his arse, jamming itself against his prostate, coupled with the working of someone's fingers around his penis. No wonder Gabriel had such an excited expression on his face, thought James.

Both boys started to moan as if they were approaching their climax. James moved his hand frantically up and down the shaft of the lad's cock and at the same time rubbed his nipples. Gabriel let out a gasp and a jet of creamy semen shot over his chest and landed just below his chin. This was followed by more spurts and the inevitable sound of Tom also arriving at his climax. James wanked the lad until there was no more juice coming out. He wiped his hands in the sticky substance and massaged it across Gabriel's stomach. It felt warm and slippery, but not as slippery as James imagined the boy's bottom must feel now Tom had spilt his load inside.

James bent forward and licked the remaining semen off Gabriel's chest and from the tip of his cock. He felt the lad shiver and could not resist putting his lips onto those of his friend and sharing the final droplets of bodily fluid with him. Their tongues wound around each other and they kissed deeply. There was a moment of total silence in the barn, undisturbed by the sound of panting or groaning.

'I think you've done very well,' said Tom, and he slipped his cock out of the lad, put it back into his breeches and took off

Gabriel's blindfold. The lad blinked violently at the light and turned around to see where everyone was. Even though he looked embarrassed, there was an excited sparkle in his eyes, and James knew that secretly he had enjoyed the experience. Tank helped to unfasten his wrists and get him down from the table, before gathering together his clothes and getting dressed.

The barn door swung open and in walked Barnaby and Sam. They both had huge grins on their faces and a conspiratorial look in their eyes. 'Have you finished?' Barnaby asked.

'Yes, thanks,' replied Tom. 'I think Gabe's ready to be part of the gang now.' The boy in question smiled as if to say he agreed and put his arm around James's shoulder.

'I bet you'll be sad to leave,' said Barnaby, as they walked back over the field and towards Sunningdale. James felt miserable, as if merely replying to his cousin's comment would mean he would have to return home sooner. He nodded sadly. 'Anyway, there's still plenty of time left. And you can always come back again next summer.'

'That's if my mother will let me,' said James.

'Oh, I'm sure she will. Just as long as you let her know just how educating it was to stay with your brilliantly gifted cousin.'

'And what wonderful paintings I did,' added James.

'Well, I wouldn't show her those if I were you, or you'll never get back to Rolvenden.' The boys all laughed, and James slipped his hand behind Gabriel's back and let it rest gently on his bottom. There was no one in sight, so it didn't matter. That was the good thing about the country, he thought, there was never anyone watching or bothering you.

There was a moment of silence when nobody seemed to know quite what to say and James whispered into Gabriel's ear, 'I like you,' and then he turned away, feeling a little embarrassed at having been so forward. The lad simply smiled and kissed him lightly on the cheek.

'I like you too,' he said.

'For goodness' sake!' exclaimed Barnaby. 'You're like a couple of girls.'

'On the contrary,' said James, 'I think I'm more man than I've ever been.'

The light was fading fast and night was about to take hold of the countryside. The boys walked slowly, side by side, enjoying the cool evening breeze. And no one said another word until they finally reached the house.

IDOL NEW BOOKS

Also published:

THE KING'S MEN
Christian Fall

Ned Medcombe, spoilt son of an Oxfordshire landowner, has always remembered his first love: the beautiful, golden-haired Lewis. But seventeenth-century England forbids such a love and Ned is content to indulge his domineering passions with the willing members of the local community, including the submissive parish cleric. Until the Civil War changes his world, and he is forced to pursue his desires as a soldier in Cromwell's army – while his long-lost lover fights as one of the King's men.

ISBN 0 352 33207 7

THE VELVET WEB
Christopher Summerisle

The year is 1889. Daniel McGaw arrives at Calverdale, a centre of academic excellence buried deep in the English countryside. But this is like no other college. As Daniel explores, he discovers secret passages in the grounds and forbidden texts in the library. The young male students, isolated from the outside world, share a darkly bizarre brotherhood based on the most extreme forms of erotic expression. It isn't long before Daniel is initiated into the rites that bind together the youths of Calverdale in a web of desire.

ISBN 0 352 33208 5

CHAINS OF DECEIT
Paul C. Alexander

Journalist Nathan Dexter's life is turned around when he meets a young student called Scott – someone who offers him the relationship for which he's been searching. Then Nathan's best friend goes missing, and Nathan uncovers evidence that he has become the victim of a slavery ring which is rumoured to be operating out of London's leather scene. To rescue their friend and expose the perverted slave trade, Nathan and Scott must go undercover, risking detection and betrayal at every turn.

ISBN 0 352 33206 9

HALL OF MIRRORS
Robert Black

Tom Jarrett operates the Big Wheel at Gamlin's Fair. When young runaway Jason Bradley tries to rob him, events are set in motion which draw the two together in a tangled web of mutual mistrust and growing fascination. Each carries a burden of old guilt and tragic unspoken history; each is running from something. But the fair is a place of magic and mystery where normal rules don't apply, and Jason is soon on a journey of self-discovery, unbridled sexuality and growing love.

ISBN 0 352 33209 3

THE SLAVE TRADE
James Masters

Barely eighteen and innocent of the desires of men, Marc is the sole survivor of a noble British family. When his home village falls to the invading Romans, he is forced to flee for his life. He first finds sanctuary with Karl, a barbarian from far-off Germanica, whose words seem kind but whose eyes conceal a dark and brooding menace. And then they are captured by Gaius, a general in Caesar's all-conquering army, in whose camp they learn the true meaning – and pleasures – of slavery.

ISBN 0 352 33228 X

DARK RIDER
Jack Gordon

While the rulers of a remote Scottish island play bizarre games of sexual dominance with the Argentinian Angelo, his friend Robert – consumed with jealous longing for his coffee-skinned companion – assuages his desires with the willing locals.

ISBN 0 352 33243 3

CONQUISTADOR
Jeff Hunter

It is the dying days of the Aztec empire. Axaten and Quetzel are members of the Stable, servants of the Sun Prince chosen for their bravery and beauty. But it is not just an honour and a duty to join this society, it is also the ultimate sexual achievement. Until the arrival of Juan, a young Spanish conquistador, sets the men of the Stable on an adventure of bondage, lust and deception.

ISBN 0 352 33244 1

WE NEED YOUR HELP . . .
to plan the future of Idol books –

Yours are the only opinions that matter. Idol is a new and exciting venture: the first British series of books devoted to homoerotic fiction for men.

We're going to do our best to provide the sexiest, best-written books you can buy. And we'd like you to help in these early stages. Tell us what you want to read. There's a freepost address for your filled-in questionnaires, so you won't even need to buy a stamp.

THE IDOL QUESTIONNAIRE

SECTION ONE: ABOUT YOU

1.1 Sex *(we presume you are male, but just in case)*
Are you?
Male	☐
Female	☐

1.2 Age
under 21	☐	21–30	☐
31–40	☐	41–50	☐
51–60	☐	over 60	☐

1.3 At what age did you leave full-time education?
still in education	☐	16 or younger	☐
17–19	☐	20 or older	☐

1.4 Occupation _____

1.5 Annual household income _____

1.6　We are perfectly happy for you to remain anonymous; but if you would like us to send you a free booklist of Idol books, please insert your name and address

_____

_____

_____

_____

SECTION TWO: ABOUT BUYING IDOL BOOKS

2.1　Where did you get this copy of *Customs of the Country*?
　　　Bought at chain book shop　☐
　　　Bought at independent book shop　☐
　　　Bought at supermarket　☐
　　　Bought at book exchange or used book shop　☐
　　　I borrowed it/found it　☐
　　　My partner bought it　☐

2.2　How did you find out about Idol books?
　　　I saw them in a shop　☐
　　　I saw them advertised in a magazine　☐
　　　I read about them in _____
　　　Other _____

2.3　Please tick the following statements you agree with:
　　　I would be less embarrassed about buying Idol
　　　books if the cover pictures were less explicit　☐
　　　I think that in general the pictures on Idol
　　　books are about right　☐
　　　I think Idol cover pictures should be as
　　　explicit as possible　☐

2.4　Would you read an Idol book in a public place – on a train for instance?
　　　Yes　☐　　　No　☐

SECTION THREE: ABOUT THIS IDOL BOOK

3.1　Do you think the sex content in this book is:
　　　Too much　☐　　About right　☐
　　　Not enough　☐

3.2 Do you think the writing style in this book is:

        Too unreal/escapist ☐   About right ☐

        Too down to earth ☐

3.3 Do you think the story in this book is:

        Too complicated ☐   About right ☐

        Too boring/simple ☐

3.4 Do you think the cover of this book is:

        Too explicit ☐   About right ☐

        Not explicit enough ☐

Here's a space for any other comments:

SECTION FOUR: ABOUT OTHER IDOL BOOKS

4.1 How many Idol books have you read?

4.2 If more than one, which one did you prefer?

        _____

4.3 Why?

SECTION FIVE: ABOUT YOUR IDEAL EROTIC NOVEL

We want to publish the books you want to read – so this is your chance to tell us exactly what your ideal erotic novel would be like.

5.1 Using a scale of 1 to 5 (1 = no interest at all, 5 = your ideal), please rate the following possible settings for an erotic novel:

        Roman / Ancient World ☐

        Medieval / barbarian / sword 'n' sorcery ☐

        Renaissance / Elizabethan / Restoration ☐

        Victorian / Edwardian ☐

        1920s & 1930s ☐

        Present day ☐

        Future / Science Fiction ☐

5.2 Using the same scale of 1 to 5, please rate the following themes you may find in an erotic novel:

Bondage / fetishism ☐
Romantic love ☐
SM / corporal punishment ☐
Bisexuality ☐
Group sex ☐
Watersports ☐
Rent / sex for money ☐

5.3 Using the same scale of 1 to 5, please rate the following styles in which an erotic novel could be written:

Gritty realism, down to earth ☐
Set in real life but ignoring its more unpleasant aspects ☐
Escapist fantasy, but just about believable ☐
Complete escapism, totally unrealistic ☐

5.4 In a book that features power differentials or sexual initiation, would you prefer the writing to be from the viewpoint of the dominant / experienced or submissive / inexperienced characters:

Dominant / Experienced ☐
Submissive / Inexperienced ☐
Both ☐

5.5 We'd like to include characters close to your ideal lover. What characteristics would your ideal lover have? Tick as many as you want:

Dominant	☐	Caring	☐
Slim	☐	Rugged	☐
Extroverted	☐	Romantic	☐
Bisexual	☐	Old	☐
Working Class	☐	Intellectual	☐
Introverted	☐	Professional	☐
Submissive	☐	Pervy	☐
Cruel	☐	Ordinary	☐
Young	☐	Muscular	☐
Naïve	☐		

Anything else? _____

5.6 Is there one particular setting or subject matter that your ideal erotic novel would contain:

_____

5.7 As you'll have seen, we include safe-sex guidelines in every book. However, while our policy is always to show safe sex in stories with contemporary settings, we don't insist on safe-sex practices in stories with historical settings because it would be anachronistic. What, if anything, would you change about this policy?

_____

_____

SECTION SIX: LAST WORDS

6.1 What do you like best about Idol books?

_____

6.2 What do you most dislike about Idol books?

_____

6.3 In what way, if any, would you like to change Idol covers?

_____

6.4 Here's a space for any other comments:

_____

_____

_____

_____

Thanks for completing this questionnaire. Now either tear it out, or photocopy it, then put it in an envelope and send it to:

Idol
FREEPOST
London
W10 5BR

You don't need a stamp if you're in the UK, but you'll need one if you're posting from overseas.